Travelling Light

Tove Jansson

Translated from the Swedish by
Silvester Mazzarella

Introduced by
Ali Smith

Other Tove Jansson titles
published by Sort Of Books

The Summer Book
A Winter Book
Fair Play
The True Deceiver

for children
The Book about Moomin, Mymble and Little My
Who Will Comfort Toffle?
The Dangerous Journey

Travelling Light (Resa Med Lätt Bagage) © Tove Jansson 1987
First published by Schildts Förlags Ab, Finland. All rights reserved
English translation © Silvester Mazzarella and Sort Of Books 2010
Introduction © Ali Smith 2010
Ali Smith and Thomas Teal provided generous help with the translation.

Thanks to Sofia Jansson for her encouragement and advice.

The illustrations on p.1 and p.208 are © Tove Jansson, 1987; the photo on
p.17 is © Tove Jansson family archive.

This English translation first published in 2010 by
Sort Of Books, PO Box 18678, London NW3 2FL.

Typeset in Goudy and GillSans to a design by Henry Iles.
Printed in Italy by Legoprint.

Sort of Books gratefully acknowledges the financial assistance of
FILI – Finnish Literature Exchange

208pp.
A catalogue record for this book is available from the British
Library

ISBN 978-0-9548995-8-5

For Tooti

Travelling
Light

Tove Jansson

014103487 1

Contents

Introduction
by Ali Smith

"Perhaps it might interest you to know what I packed? As
little as possible! I've always dreamed of travelling light, a
small weekend bag of the sort one can casually whisk along
with oneself as one walks with rapid but unhurried steps
through, shall we say, the departure lounge of an airport,
passing a mass of nervous people dragging along large
heavy cases."

There's something tragically doomed – and comically too –
in the determined light-heartedness of the main character
in the title story of *Travelling Light* as he steps out, carrying
"the absolute minimum". No more emotional baggage for
him, he decides. No more listening to, and by implication
becoming responsible for, the fears and anxieties of others.
Instead, he'll maintain a pure and optimistic disconnection,
pass through the modern world with a sweet and
lightweight sense of solitude. He won't listen to anybody's
needs; he won't be encumbered by anybody's story.

But what this story reveals is that there's no such thing
as disconnection; and it does this in its very form, not
just in the funny, sad unfolding of its plot. "Believe me,
you can't imagine my giddy sense of freedom". In the

very act of announcing how determined he is to go solo,
this man is already helplessly accompanied – by "you", in
other words, us, listening to him. Tove Jansson's sleight of
hand means that his freedom – and our own – is already
disturbingly and laughingly compromised.

At the heart of *Travelling Light* is Jansson's insistence that
no man or woman is an island. No matter how much we
may long to escape others, we can't; and even the simplest
daily act of existing in the world, living with others, never
mind anything more intimate, is fraught with alienation.
The collection revels in this paradox, the human longing
for solitude versus the human need for contact. Can you
travel light? What happens to this urge when it's dark?
Its very funny stories are deadly serious; its world is one
in a state of fragmentation and breakdown, sometimes
obvious, sometimes covert, but breakdown at all levels
from intimate to global. In a series of surreal encounters
which, on the one hand, gently nudge a reader out of
any comfort zone and, on the other, deliberately smash
notions of comfort into shiny broken shards, the collection
is a work of fusion, of entertainment with disquietude,
exhilaration with resignation. The stories ask questions
about inclusion and exclusion, insiders and outsiders; they
ricochet between the polar opposites of sea and land,
island and mainland, foreignness and familiarity, past and
future, youth and age, each one a kind of journey in itself, a
symbiosis of light and dark.

Travelling Light – *Resa Med Lätt Bagage* in its original
Swedish title – was Jansson's fourth collection of short stories
for adults; she published it in 1987, when she was seventy-
three. Her first book for adults had been the short-story
collection *Sculptor's Daughter*, published in 1968; she would
write five more collections before her death in 2001 at
the age of eighty-six. In her lifetime, her international fame

came as the writer and illustrator for children of the Finn
Family Moomintroll, whose cheerful, day-to-day, open-
natured philosophy and benign inclusivity ensures their
survival, and that of everybody round them, in the deepest,
darkest, most existential of Scandinavian landscapes. Now,
as the work to which she devoted more than thirty years
of her later life is being made available in English at long
last, this earlier fame is steadily being matched by a fast-
growing international appreciation of her light-footed,
deep-resonating writing for adults. Very excitingly, there's
still a fair amount to come, in memoir, novel and short
story form, and each new translation proves a revelation
of Jansson's literary astuteness, liberating philosophical
understanding and aesthetic generosity.

The Fredrikson family, in the hilarious, unsettling "The
Summer Child', consider themselves very generous; they
have openly advertised for a child from the city to come
and spend the summer in their idyllic rural setting with
them, for a small fee. The child who arrives is apocalyptic,
"anything but childlike". In a story which challenges the
ways we narrate ourselves, the family saddles itself with
Elis, a gloomy little conscience "well informed about
everything that's dying and miserable", who makes them
feel guilty about everything, from not eating their leftovers
to global pollution, and pierces them with his human
oddness; the story, a fable of innocence and knowledge,
becomes about the very act of discomfiting others, the
moral attraction and the powermongering of it. It has
something of the nature of an unexploded mine about it,
as does the psychologically-loaded "The Woman Who
Borrowed Memories", where an artist revisits her "starry-
eyed" past; and when this past, in the form of a suffocating
old friend, threatens to devour both what she was then
and is now, even to write her out of her own life story,

Tove Jansson's artwork for the original Swedish publication
of *Resa Med Lätt Bagage (Travelling Light)*, 1987

she learns exactly why we move on, why nostalgia is deathly, why we can't and mustn't go backwards in life.

Into this heady, psychologically dizzying story, at just the right moment, comes a defusing line like this one: "the spring evening came into the room, cool and liberating". These are stories whose interruptions and moments of change are crucial; stories made, themselves, to interrupt things both liberatingly and much more darkly, just as "The PE Teacher's Death" interrupts its characters' dinner-party fashionable superficialia with a death, a suicide right in the middle of things, and one that seems more meaningful, more committed to life even in the death, than the lives its characters find themselves living.

Travelling Light is also a book about the existential landscape of old age – though, as Jansson has one character point out, "there's not as much difference as people think between the young and the old". "A Foreign City", one of her most unassuming and powerful stories, sees old age as a Kafkaesque desolate cityscape where "words disappear as easily as hats, as easily as faces and names." But what starts as a story of bumbling ineptitude soon transforms into one about a much more endangering and dangerous state; in the end the fundaments of communication and the restoration of lost meaning to things – and to people – become the only route of escape and survival.

Each of the three very short stories in *Travelling Light* – "A Foreign City", "The Gulls" and "The Forest" – is a masterpiece of brevity. "The Gulls" is a deeply-layered tiny tale of lifeforce and murderous powerplay and possessiveness; "The Forest" an almost casual anatomising of why storytelling matters. Jansson insists throughout this collection, perhaps even more than she usually does in her writing, that landscape is never not psychological,

that landscape and pyschology are vitally connected.
Throughout *Travelling Light*, as throughout all her work,
she examines why art and narrative matter to us, how and
why they're part of the human condition. But in particular,
in this collection, she highlights social preconception and
imprisoning judgementalism, and how art and narrative
partly offer open doors out of both and are partly
themselves preconditioned by both. In the opening story,
"An Eightieth Birthday", the young, naive protagonists, new
to life and love, worry desperately about being "the right
kind of person", being seen to understand "the right kind
of art". The real artists, though, are the dishevelled, stained
outsiders, past their best, "critiqued long ago", and the
old woman whose birthday they're celebrating, a survivor
stubborn enough always to have painted trees no matter
what the aesthetic fashion was, "till in the end she knew
trees, the very essence of trees." Out walking in the middle
of the night with the disreputable old artists, May sees for
the first time how very beautiful the city she lives in is.

This is recognisable Jansson territory; the simple,
essential connection, between seeing and thinking,
becomes central to the art of these stories. But the
collection's bravery lies in its radical consideration of the
failures of words, of the cold-shouldering art can involve,
the disconsolations of art. In fact, when it comes to both
art and life, the stories are uncompromising and truthful
about an inevitable disconsolation.

There is an urgency in the writing, a warning about
not leaving things too late. Seeing a tree in bloom, seeing
it in front of her eyes as if for the first time, "it suddenly
occurred" to May "that I hadn't loved Jonny the way I could
have loved him, totally." *Travelling Light* is passionate about
trees and meadows, teems with unexpected, out-of-place
Tarzans and jungles, teems with nature in all its seemingly

tamed and uncontrollable forms. It is repeatedly coruscating about modern homogenous and desolate landscapes, fake and "flat and featureless apart from recurring groups of high-rise blocks set at an angle to the road, and petrol stations, all the ordinary roadside places, all the same, without character, monotonous as polite conversation". In this collection Jansson has no time for politeness. She meets these paucity-revealing landscapes head-on with a lifeforce so huge and full and wild that things are bound to be explosive in the collision. But at the same time, she insists, there's nothing romantic about trying to embrace this lifeforce, and there's no such place as "The Isle of Bliss ... so far away nothing dangerous can get to it".

In this lies the collection's other source of fruitful collision, between so-called romantic isolation and troubled human interaction. In "The Garden of Eden", Viktoria, an elderly professor, arrives at an empty house in a place wholly foreign to her, opens a door on a totally new landscape and uncovers the same old colonising layers of judgementalism and powerplay as exist everywhere. She can't not become implicated in the multilayered social interactions even in this tiny Spanish village. Her new way with old stories, her new perception about the ways in which we construct narratives about ourselves and others, opens doors on a very old story of her own, in a way that's tragically too little, too late yet still full of a healing kind of release.

How typical of Tove Jansson, that a book which deals with such darknesses, such weighty matters, a collection so consistently concerned with people, relationships and societies in states of breakdown, at the ends of their tethers, even apocalyptically ruined, unfixably fragmented, should be one of her funniest, most unpindownably airy works. In effect it creates its funniness, and equally its sadness, out of the impossibility of detachment, the struggle for proper connection, and the surreality of both. These are stories quietly, unsensationally, going out of their way to disconcert their readers, "get them out of their tight little cliques" so they'll "listen and understand each other a little better", as Viktoria puts it, thinking of her own aim in getting two troubled people together in the hope that they'll hear each other before it's too late. "Ladies, you waste your time on inessentials. When we've finished our coffee, I think we should devote ourselves to the contemplation of nightfall".

The final piece, "Correspondence", is a story stripped back to essentials. It's one of the closest of Jansson's works to autobiography, a story she constructed out of the letters sent to her by a young Japanese admirer of her books. This paradoxically makes it a story which includes us too – makes it directly about the relationship of Jansson's reader, the person holding this copy of *Travelling Light* in his or her hand, to Jansson herself, the writer of all the stories that have come before it. Its inclusion makes it a direct gift to us individual readers: a commentary on the paradoxical joint intimacy and solitude in the act of reading (and writing).

An interweaving of real excitement, real poetry and real loss; a story of youth and age and the limitations of both; it spells out, beautifully, through one writer's generosity in using the words of another, the terrible alienation love reveals, the distance inherent in intimacy. It becomes a fable of what human beings can and can't give each other. It is full of a pure love and a haunting longing. The demands of these are huge, beautiful, terrifying, unacceptable. More: something of these demands, she suggests, sits at the core of any narrative. "I can't write my story without you."

How lightly Jansson's fiction traverses the wide world. How profoundly it implicates us.

Tove Jansson in Japan, 1971, with Tuulikki Pietilä (left)

Travelling
Light

An Eightieth Birthday

WHEN WE ARRIVED and Jonny caught sight of the big cars parked outside Grandma's building, he said right away that he should have worn a dark suit.

"Don't be silly, sweetheart," I said. "Relax. Grandma isn't like that. People pop in and out in corduroy trousers and all sorts of stuff. She likes bohemians."

"But that's just it," he said. "I'm no bohemian, I'm ordinary. I've no right to wear corduroys to an eightieth birthday party. And I've never even met her before."

I said, "We'll unwrap it before we go in, it's more polite. Grandma doesn't like opening parcels, except at Christmas."

Choosing the present hadn't been easy. Grandma rang up and said, "Dear child, make sure you bring your young man so I can have a look at him, but don't go buying some expensive and unnecessary gift. At my age, I've got pretty much everything I want, plus better taste than most of my progeny. And I don't want to leave a load of rubbish for others to clean up after I'm gone. Just pick out something simple and affectionate. And don't go bringing art into it – you'll only mess it up."

We racked our brains. Grandma thinks of herself as so broad-minded and easygoing, but in fact she's forever burdening the family with modest requests which, in all their simplicity, can be a real pain. It would have been easy, for example, to choose her a stylish bowl in thick glass, but no, that would have been too bourgeois and not at all affectionate.

Of course, I'd told Jonny all about Grandma and her paintings, and he was really impressed. We have one of her early sketches at home, a drawing of San Gimignano, where she went on her first grant-funded trip, before she became famous for painting trees. She often talked about San Gimignano and I always loved hearing her talk about how happy she was in that little Italian town with all its towers; how strong and free she felt when she used to wake up at dawn to work, and a signorina would push her vegetable cart through the streets and Grandma would open her window and point at what she wanted and they would understand each other perfectly and laugh, and it was hot and everything was incredibly cheap, and then Grandma would set off with her easel...

It's a story Jonny likes, too. And then, would you believe it, the other day Jonny went off on his own and found a picture of San Gimignano in a little second-hand shop! So that's our present. They said in the shop it was an early nineteenth-century lithograph. We didn't think it was that special, but anyway.

"Jonny," I said. "Let's go in now. Just be yourself, act natural, that's what she likes."

There was a long line of well-wishers queuing in the doorway of Grandma's studio. A couple of young cousins were scampering in and out, taking everyone's coats, and we were gradually swept into the large, airy room, beautifully decorated by Grandma's acolytes. I fixed my sights on her and steered us forward, giving Jonny's arm a quick squeeze to calm him. In the background some low music was playing – not classical, but something specially chosen, bearing Grandma's personal stamp. We walked towards her. She had dressed with her usual studied nonchalance; her white hair lightly arranged in casual curls around her watchful, gracious face and clear, teasing eyes.

"This is Jonny," I said. "Jonny, Grandma."

"How nice of you to come," Grandma said. "So this is Jonny. Finnish-speaking, I believe?" She smiled at him benignly. "How will you cope in an ossified old family where no one speaks anything but Swedish? And how are things, are you two married or not? All done and dusted?"

"Done but not dusted," said Jonny boldly. Grandma laughed and I knew she liked him.

"Well, where's your present?"

She stared at the picture of San Gimignano for a long time, remarked that we'd gone to a great deal of trouble, and flashed a quick smile. "I drew that same view," she said, "but better." Then, with a little gesture that was dismissive but also showed a secret understanding, she moved on.

The large table on which Grandma posed her models dominated the room. It was covered with her brocade from Barcelona and richly spread with everything from olives to cream cakes. Young family members ran about with vases they'd filled with water earlier that morning, while people stood about in groups having frenetic conversations and everyone was served a glass of champagne. Grandma sailed above all this like in a painting by Chagall, dispensing a sort of general benediction as she moved about the room dropping small pronouncements here and there. But I noticed she took care not to introduce anyone by name. Not the slightest suggestion of failing memory – just introduce yourselves, dear friends. Oh, to be as free as Grandma!

A mass of screaming children persisted in running back and forth across the studio, but this didn't seem to irritate Grandma in the least. She just let the mothers take charge of whoever it was they had brought into the world. Jonny and I sat down at a crowded table only to realise a moment too late that we'd chosen badly. This was a table for what Grandma calls the intellectuals, who associate exclusively with one another. I couldn't figure out what they were talking about. Despairing of something to say, and after a long silence, I finally turned to a gentleman with a goatee and remarked that the evening light in the studio was unusually beautiful. To my relief, he started talking about the significance of light and then moved on to the theory of perception. It took me ages to work out that he was an art critic.

Luckily all he seemed to want was a listener, so I nodded thoughtfully and said yes of course, and how true, and occasionally glanced at Jonny, who was sitting across from me looking miserable. He'd got stuck beside one of those geniuses who never say a word to help you out. Even so, I was quite proud of having brought my Jonny into a family with artistic roots, who really knew how to carry off a party on this scale.

Eventually he extricated himself and came over and hissed in my ear, "Can we go home now?"

"Of course," I said. "Soon."

It was then that they came in, three gentlemen of uncertain appearance. They looked somehow dishevelled – or, more accurately, stained or smudged. They certainly weren't bohemians. They did have long hair, but in a more middle-aged way. They made a grand entrance, bowing low to Grandma and kissing her hand. She led them to an empty table at the far end near the window and made sure each got a glass of champagne. Pretty soon one of them dropped his glass on the floor. He was in a state about it, but Grandma just smiled, though I knew how much she treasured those glasses – a wedding-present, I think. Coffee and cake were being brought in now, but these new gentlemen continued to be served champagne. Not the rest of us.

I noticed Jonny was cleverly moving along the wall by carefully studying everything hanging on it, till in the end he reached the new gentlemen's table. Of course he didn't understand that this was a table set aside for the not-entirely-respectable; dear, sweet Jonny. But he did seem to be enjoying himself at last.

One of the three went over and lifted a whole bottle of whisky from the liquor table and, as he carried it back, made a deep bow to Grandma, whose smile seemed to be wearing a little thin.

My art critic had moved a bit further off but was still delivering an animated lecture about the theory of perception. I got up quietly and snuck over to Jonny, because it depressed me listening to stuff I didn't really understand or care about. One of the gentlemen, with a droopy grey moustache, lifted his glass and said, "And so he writes crap about you, Juksu."

"Absolutely," said Juksu. "And only three inches."

"You measured it?"

"Of course, I took out my ruler and I measured. Exactly three inches. Like buying pea soup in a plastic bag, so you know what you're getting. And no picture. But these newcomers, they get a picture, by God."

The third man said, "The trouble is, he's so old; he just panders to the young."

"Yes, it's hell."

"But you can't have everything in life," said the man with the moustache.

"No."

They talked on, calmly and thoughtfully. They sounded like men who were used to talking together but could no longer be bothered with actual discussions. They made statements. They never referred to things like perception but seemed more interested in rising rents or an unfair review of some painting, though of course what could you expect... But when Grandma passed by on one of her charming circuits of the room, they grew lively and gallant. Jonny said not a word, but I could see he was fascinated. None of them paid us much attention, though they made sure our glasses were always full and made a space for me closer to the table. Their conversation was soothing, and we sat as if on an island sanctuary. None of them asked us about ourselves; they let us be anonymous.

The party around us floated into the distance. The room had grown dim; the children had vanished. Suddenly someone turned on the overhead light and someone else carried in pirogi. The man called Juksu stood up. So did the rest of us, and somehow we all came out into the hall together. After a lot of bowing and scraping and sincere expressions of affection for Grandma, we took the lift down. But Grandma managed to whisper to me, "Don't buy them drinks. There are three of them and you can't afford it." Though I think she saw that Juksu had her whisky bottle hidden inside his coat.

* * *

It was cold when we came out on the street. And very quiet. No cars or people and that remarkable half-light that comes with spring evenings. After a fairly long silence we introduced ourselves. They were Keke and Juksu and the one with the moustache was Vilhelm.

"Well, let's get going," said Vilhelm. "We'll head into town. But not to the usual place."

"No," said Keke. "Not there. They're not nice any more. Let's go sit down somewhere and then we'll see." Then he turned to me and said, in a very kind voice, "How long have you two been living together?"

"Two months," I said. "Well, two and a half, nearly."

"And it's going well?"

"Oh yes, really well."

Vilhelm said, "Let's go to our spot. Where the newspapers are."

This was outside the covered market down by the harbour. We each took a newspaper to sit on out of a recycling bin and settled in a line along the edge of the quay. The square was empty.

"Now let's have a little drink," said Juksu to Jonny. "But we'll have to do without glasses, if your wife will excuse us. You don't say much. Everything okay?"

"Just fine," said Jonny.

I had a feeling I ought to go and let him stay there with the three of them. I turned to Vilhelm and said politely, "It's really nice here. I like people who don't take life so seriously."

"You're very young," said Vilhelm. "But you have a wonderful grandmother."

We had a drink together and then suddenly Jonny spoke up excitedly. "I was listening to what you were saying, that we can't expect to have everything in life, but still you have to expect something, I mean expect something incredible, from yourself and from other people… You have to set your sights high because it always turns out a little lower, if you know what I mean – like with a bow and arrow…"

"That's it exactly," said Keke reassuringly. "You're absolutely right. Look, here they come. I like boats."

We took another swig from the bottle as we watched the fishing-boats slowly approach the quay. Two drunks wandered up. "Hi, Keke," said one of them. "Oh sorry, you've got company. Got any cigarettes?"

Keke gave each of them a cigarette and they walked on. Up in the spring sky the dome of the cathedral rested like a white dream over the empty square. Helsinki was indescribably beautiful, I'd never realised before how beautiful it was.

"The Nikolai Church," said Juksu. "They have to change everything. So now they call it the Great Church. It's idiotic, it doesn't mean anything." He let the empty bottle slide into the water and said as a kind of afterthought that they can't even write decent poetry any more.

By now the night was as dark as it ever gets in May, but we still didn't need any lights.

"Tell me something," I said. "What do they mean by perception?"

"Observation," said Vilhelm. "You see something and suddenly you recognise some old idea or, better yet, some new idea."

"Yes," said Keke. "A new idea."

I was feeling cold and suddenly angry and said eightieth birthday parties were a really stupid idea.

"My dear," said Vilhelm. "It was a proper party, and a beautiful one in its way, but now it's over. Now there's just us sitting here trying to think."

"What about?" said Juksu.

"About ourselves. About everything."

"What do you suppose Grandma's thinking about?"

"No one knows."

Vilhelm went on. "For instance, about this business of maybe fifty a week. They run themselves ragged. And still they only have time for the young ones, the bastards."

"Who?" I asked.

"The art critics. Fifty shows a week."

"And no one asks any more," Keke said. "We're over and done with. We were critiqued long ago." He thought for a moment. "My bum's getting cold. Let's make a move."

As we walked further along the quayside, he asked me what I wanted from life.

I hesitated. Then I said, "Love. Security, maybe?"

"Of course," he said. "That's right. In a way – for you at least."

"And travel," I added. "I've got this real passion to travel."

Keke was quiet for a while and then he said, "Passion. As you can see, I've lived quite a long time, which is to say I've been working for quite a long time, which is the same thing. And you know what? In the whole silly business, the only thing that really matters is passion. It comes and it goes. At first it just comes to you free of charge, and you don't understand, and you waste it. And then it becomes a thing to nurture."

It was awfully cold. He was walking too slowly, and I was freezing.

Then he said, "You lose sight of the picture. I think we're out of cigarettes."

"Not a bit of it," said Juksu. "Philip Morris – Grandma shoved them in my pocket. She knows what it's like."

Keke went over to the other two men. They lit their cigarettes and walked on as slowly as before.

Jonny and I followed them. I whispered, "Are you tired of this? You want to go home?"

"Ssh," he said. "I want to hear what they're saying."

"His clay," Vilhelm was saying. "It went to an amateur. Some pushy little nobody. He hadn't been dead two days when this creep comes along and buys the clay from his widow for nothing. And he was old; just imagine that clay."

"Hang on a minute, Jonny," I said. "I've got sand in my shoes." But Jonny went on ahead with the others.

When he came back he told me excitedly how clay becomes more and more a living thing over time and how you always use the same clay for every sculpture and you can't ever let it dry out, and new clay just isn't the same, it's not alive…

I asked him which of them was the actual sculptor, but he didn't know.

"They were just talking about seeing a picture," he said, "so I don't know." But he was very excited and asked if we had anything at home, anything we could offer them. After all, it wasn't that late. "And anyway," Jonny said, "this isn't a chance we'll ever have again. I really want to."

I knew we didn't have much in the house, and Jonny knew it too, perfectly well. Some anchovies, bread and butter and cheese, but only one bottle of red wine.

"That's enough," said Jonny. "You and I can just pretend to drink. They'll stay for a while, long enough, don't you think? And it's only just around the corner."

"Okay, let's do it," I said, and he laughed.

Brunnspark was beautiful: everything growing and bursting into leaf. Suddenly I wasn't tired any more; all I knew was that Jonny was happy.

We all stopped in front of a large bird-cherry tree that was already in full bloom, shining chalk-white in the spring night. As I looked at the tree, it suddenly occurred to me that I hadn't loved Jonny the way I could have loved him, totally.

Keke looked at me and said, "That's only a gift; it doesn't mean anything."

I didn't understand. We walked on.

He said, "You know your grandmother never painted anything but trees, and always trees in the same park. In the end she knew trees, the very essence of trees. She's very strong. She never lost her passion."

Of course I had huge respect for these men who did nothing but search for their lost passion and cared about nothing else, but at the same time I was worried there wasn't enough coffee and the house was a mess. And I started thinking about what was on our walls; maybe our pictures were completely unacceptable, just things we liked without having any idea why. Keke asked me if I was cold.

"No," I said, "One more street and we'll be home."

"Your grandmother," said Keke, "has she ever talked to you about her work?"

"No, she never has."

"Good," Keke said, "that's good. They wrote her off in the sixties but she stuck to her guns. You know, my dear – I'm sorry, what's your name?"

"May," I said.

"Perfect. You know, it was all Informalism then, everywhere; everyone was supposed to paint the same way." He looked at me and could see I didn't understand. "Informalism means, roughly, painting without using definite forms, just colour. What happened was that a lot of old, very talented artists hid away in their studios and tried to paint like young people. They were afraid of being left behind. Some managed to do it, more or less, and others got lost and never found their way back. But your grandmother stuck to her own style and it was still there when all that other stuff had had its day. She was brave, or maybe stubborn."

I said, very carefully, "Or maybe she could only paint her own way?"

"Marvellous," said Keke. "She simply had no choice. You comfort me."

We'd come to the door of our building, and I said, "Now we have to be quiet or the neighbours will complain. Jonny, you go up and get something out of the fridge – whatever you can find."

We got in. Jonny put out the red wine and glasses and our guests sat down and went on with their conversation.

We didn't turn on the lamp; there was enough light from the window.

After a bit Jonny said he had something they might like to see, and I knew he wanted to show them his model ship. He's been working on it for a couple of years, every detail handmade. So they went into the spare room and Jonny switched on the overhead light. I could hear a murmur of conversation but left them in peace and went to the pantry to put on some coffee.

By and by, Jonny came out into our little kitchen. "They said I've got a passion," he whispered. "A vision of my own." He was very agitated. "But it's not theirs, it's not the one they're searching for."

"Great!" I said. "You take in the coffee and I'll bring the rest."

When I came out, Vilhelm was talking about the flowering bird cherry we'd seen on the way home. He said, "What can you do with something like that?"

"Just let it flower," said Keke. "Look, here's our lovely hostess! Isn't that right – shouldn't we just let it flower and admire it? It's one way to live. Trying to recreate it is another. That's what it boils down to."

After the party broke up, Jonny was silent till we went to bed. Then he said, "Maybe my passion is nothing special, but at least it's mine."

"It is that," I said.

The Summer Child

IT WAS CLEAR from the very start that nobody at Backen liked him. He was a thin, gloomy child of eleven, who somehow always looked hungry. The boy should have aroused people's most tender protective instincts, but he just didn't. Partly it was his way of looking at people or, rather, of observing them, with a suspicious piercing stare that was anything but childlike. And then he would hold forth in his odd precocious way, and dear God the things he came out with!

It would have been easier to overlook all this if Elis had come from a poor home, but he did not. His clothes and his suitcase were clearly expensive and his father's car had delivered him to the ferry landing. It had all been arranged by advert and telephone: the Fredrikson family were offering a holiday home to a child for the summer out of the goodness of their hearts, and for a small fee, of course. Axel and Hanna had discussed it thoroughly – all the big-city children in need of fresh air, woods, water, and good food. They had said all the things people usually say to convince themselves that only one course of action would allow them to sleep easily at night. Meanwhile there was all the rest of the work that had to be done in June. Many of the summer residents' boats were still on their slips and a couple of them hadn't even been properly checked over.

And so the boy arrived, carrying a bunch of roses for his hostess.

"You really didn't need to, Elis," said Hanna, thanking him. "Or was it your mother who sent them?"

"No, Mrs Fredrikson," Elis answered. "My mother's remarried. It was my father who bought them."

"Very kind of him... But couldn't he have waited a little before driving off?"

"I'm afraid not, an important conference. He sends his respects."

"Yes, yes, right," said Axel Fredrikson. "Well, let's get aboard and get home. The kids can't wait to meet you. That's quite a suitcase you've got there."

Elis told them it had cost eight hundred and fifty marks.

Axel's boat was quite large, a sturdy fishing-boat with a deckhouse, and he'd built it himself. The boy climbed awkwardly aboard and at the first splash of spray he grabbed hold of the seat and closed his eyes tight.

"Axel, don't drive so fast," said Hanna.

"He can go in the deckhouse."

But Elis wouldn't let go of the seat or even once look out at the sea the whole way there.

The children were waiting expectantly on the dock – Tom, Oswald and little Camilla, whom they all called Mia.

"Well," said Axel. "This is Elis. He's about the same age as Tom, so you should get on fine."

Elis stepped onto the dock, went up to Tom, took his hand, gave a short bow and said his full name: "Elis Gräsbäck". Then he did the same with Oswald, but just looked at Mia, who giggled uncontrollably and put her hands over her mouth. They walked up to the cottage, Axel carrying the suitcase while Hanna carried a basket of shopping from the local store. She put on the water for coffee; the sandwiches were already made. The children sat round the table staring at Elis.

"Just help yourselves," Hanna urged them. "Elis is new here, so he can go first."

Elis half stood up, took a sandwich with a sort of little bow, and said it was remarkably hot for the time of year. The children continued to goggle at him as if bewitched and Mia said, "Mum? Why's he like that?"

"Ssh," said Hanna. "Elis, please help yourself to some salmon. We caught four on Thursday."

Elis stood halfway up again and observed that it was remarkable you could still find salmon when the water was so polluted. Then he told them what salmon cost in town, meaning of course for those who could afford to eat salmon outside of special occasions. Somehow he made them all uncomfortable.

In the evening, when Tom went to empty the slop pail into the bay, Elis followed and saw what he did and talked on and on about the polluted oceans and how irresponsible people were destroying the whole world.

"He's weird," Tom said. "You can't talk to him. He just talks nonstop about pollution and how much everything costs."

"Ignore it," said Hanna. "He's our guest."

"Weird sort of guest! He follows me round all the time!"

It was quite true. Wherever Tom went, Elis was right behind: the boathouse, the fishing beach, the woodpile, absolutely everywhere.

"What are you doing now?"

"Making a bailer dipper, obviously."

"Why don't you have plastic bailers?"

"Just what we need," said Tom contemptuously. "This dipper's going to be a special shape, and it'll take me a while to make it."

Elis accepted this and said seriously, "Of course. What with decorating it, as well. But it's such a waste of good work."

"What do you mean?"

"I mean, since the world's going to end, you might as well use plastic."

And then he'd start in again, the whole thing, nuclear war and God knows what, blah, blah, blah, nothing but endless blather.

Their room was in the attic over the kitchen, with a sloping roof and a window that looked out toward the meadow. In the evening Elis would take ages folding his clothes and hanging them up, placing his right shoe properly next to the left and winding up his wristwatch.

"Yes, but what's the point of all that?" Tom said. "You said a nuclear war could happen any minute, even tomorrow. Then it's all down the drain with Friberg's gherkins."

"Friberg's gherkins?"

"It's just a saying."

"Why? Who's Friberg?"

"Lie down and go to sleep and stop being stupid. I don't feel like talking."

Elis turned to the wall. His silence was compact, but you knew very well what he was thinking, and you knew that little by little it would all come out, there was no stopping it, and come it did, a soft-spoken litany about the ruined sea and the ruined air and then all the wars and all the people who had nothing to eat and were dying everywhere all the time and what can we do, what can we do...

Tom sat up in bed and said, "But that's all a million miles away. Come on, what's really up with you?"

"I don't know," said Elis, adding after a while, "don't be angry with me."

Then, at last, silence.

* * *

Tom was used to being the eldest and making decisions and giving orders to Oswald and Mia and sorting out the silly things they did; it was just what older brothers do. But for some reason it was different with Elis; totally impossible to get any sense into him even though he was the same age as Tom. You just got angry with him. It didn't even feel good when he admired you. And it was all so unfair. Like that business with the grebe. It wasn't Tom's fault the bird got stuck in the net. These things happen. He threw it in the water and Elis made a big deal out of it. "Tom. That grebe took a long time to die. They can dive tens of metres deep. Did you know that? Think how she must have felt, how long she must have tried to hold her breath..."

"You're crazy," Tom said, but it made him feel bad.

Or he might say, "I know what you do with kittens, you drown them. Do you have any idea...?" And on and on – it was unbearable.

Elis buried the grebe up near the road to the town where there had been a forest fire and there was nothing left among the tree stumps but willowherb; trust him to find a spot like that. He put up a cross with a number on it. Number one. Other graves followed – rat-trap victims, birds that had flown into windows, poisoned field mice, all solemnly buried and numbered. Sometimes Elis would remark in passing about all the lonely graves that had no one to care for them. "And where is your own family graveyard? I'm interested. Do you have a lot of relatives buried there?"

When it came to giving people a bad conscience, he was an expert. Sometimes all he had to do was just look at you with those gloomy, grown-up eyes and you would instantly be reminded of all your failings.

One day, when Elis's forebodings were even gloomier than usual, Hanna cut him off. "You're very well-informed about everything that's dying and miserable, aren't you, Elis?"

"I have to be," he answered seriously. "No one else cares."

For a moment Hanna was overcome by goodness knows what and wanted to take the child in her arms and hug him, but his stern gaze stopped her. "I shouldn't be so hard on him," she told herself later. "I must be kinder." But before she had the chance, something terrible and unforgivable happened. Elis promised to give little Mia three Finnish marks to show him her bottom. "He wanted to watch me pee," said Mia. And, almost as bad, Elis asked his landlord, "How much are you getting for me?"

"What did you say?"

"How much a month are you being paid for me? Is it over the counter? I mean, are you paying tax on it?"

Axel exchanged a look with his wife and left the kitchen.

On top of all this, Elis had a real talent for finding things that were broken. He was constantly dragging in damaged items and showing them to Tom. "Can you fix this? You can fix anything. Look, it's been out in the rain and it's gone all mouldy. It was nice, once."

"Chuck it out," said Tom. "I only make new things. I can't be bothered with rubbish."

Elis collected the junk in a pile beside his cemetery. The pile got bigger and bigger and he seemed almost proud of his sad collection. No one else ever noticed all the worn-out, useless junk scattered on the hill. They simply didn't see it. But Elis did, with his sharp, critical eye. Sometimes when he fixed the family with that look of his, they would suddenly become conscious that their work clothes were filthy, and their hands.

One time Hanna spoke to him with a bit of authority, "Elis, please, just eat your dinner and stop agonising about everything. Put a little flesh on your bones so your father won't be ashamed of you when he collects you in the autumn."

Elis said, "You mean you'll be able to put up with me until the autumn?" When no one said anything, he went on. "You waste an awful lot of food. Do you never think about all the people in the world who have no food at all? I'm sorry to have to say it, but I know what you throw away and how it all ends up in the sea."

"That's enough!" Axel burst out and got up from the table. "I'm going outside to look at the boats."

Admittedly the Fredriksons were a bit spoiled. They didn't like food unless it was absolutely fresh, whether fish or meat or Hanna's home-baked bread, so a great deal did wind up down the drain with Friberg's pickles, as the saying goes. Elis discovered this fact at once. He would go to the fridge and take out the leftovers that usually lay there until they were stale enough to be thrown away with a clear conscience. He would carefully rescue these remnants and eat them. He might say, for instance, "No meatballs, thank you. The old fish soup is fine for me."

"Ha ha," said Oswald, who followed most of what was happening and thought about it, and who never had his brother to himself any more because of the summer child. "Ha ha. You're our new slop pail, aren't you?"

"We eat what we eat," Axel said. "But it's not good manners to comment on what our guests eat. Food is not something we discuss. It's just a fact of life."

"It most certainly is not," Elis objected. "Think of all the poor people who don't..." But that was as far as he got, because Axel banged his hand on the table and said, "Now you be quiet! And the rest of you, too. There's no peace in this house any more."

Out of doors, though, all was completely at peace. It was a time of light breezes and soft summer rain; down in the meadow the apple trees were in bloom, and all of nature was at its loveliest. In previous summers, Tom had wandered the woods and along the shore through the bright summer nights, but it was no fun this year. He could never count on being alone.

"Mum," he said. "How long is he staying?"

"People come and people go," Hanna answered. "Relax. There's a time for everything. This, too, will pass."

The worst part was that Elis was able to support all his arguments with incontrovertible statistics. Whenever the news came on, he glued his ear to the radio to collect new miseries or get the old ones confirmed. The news was the only programme he cared about. But he would sometimes mix actual catastrophes with his own fantasies, which then wormed their way so deeply into his dreadful prophecies that Tom didn't know which way was up.

With Elis around, you had to be constantly ready for the worst. For example, Granny was a long-term patient in the local hospital, but when Elis came in and said, "She just died!" it turned out it wasn't Granny he meant, but a crow with one leg, for heaven's sake, that he'd been caring for all week.

One day when Hanna was taking the bus to go and see her mother, Elis asked if he could come along, and she thought why not. Of course he was a morbid child, but he did have great compassion for any creature in distress.

The experiment was not repeated. Granny didn't care for all the sighing and groaning at her bedside. He shook his head mournfully and pressed her hand as if saying a final farewell, and when he went out for a few minutes, she asked Hanna angrily, "Who's this insufferable child you've dragged along?"

There was no getting around the fact that the summer child was affecting everyone in the house. They were all a little afraid of him. Axel no longer smoked his pipe after meals but he stomped straight off to the boathouse. He'd grown sullen, and one day when Elis started inter-rogating him about his income and political views, he stood up and walked out in the middle of the fish soup. Little Mia was too small and innocent to understand, but she sensed the change and grew whiny and difficult. As for Oswald, he was openly jealous. Tom had no time for him any more, and when they did go out fishing together it wasn't in the nice old friendly, peaceful way. Oswald developed a biting irony: "Are you really going to murder that poor little cod?" or "Look how many corpses in the net today!" And so forth. The whole family had fallen on evil days.

Axel and Hanna knew they'd put a terrible burden on Tom with this summer child, but what could they do?

They had their hands full with their daily chores and the kids pretty much had to look out for themselves.

One day, Axel said, "Tom, forget about splitting that firewood, please, and go keep an eye on Elis."

"I'd rather split wood. But he'll be around my neck in any case, so what difference does it make?" "Well, do what you want," said Axel helplessly and started to walk away, then turned back and said, "I'm so sorry about all this."

You think you're taking in an underprivileged child from the city, but no, you're saddling yourselves with an implacably critical observer who never lets up about the wickedness and sorrows of the world. Do people in the city all raise their kids to view the world with suspicion? Do they all burden them with a conscience they're too young to understand or manage? Axel discussed it with his wife and she thought maybe they did. The boy needed a change. Why not take him out on the water a bit, now the weather was so calm and beautiful? Hanna could use the time to visit some of her relatives in Lovisa, and Axel had to take some gas canisters out to the lighthouses in any case. The Coast Guard office had phoned that very morning to say the beacon at Västerbåda had gone out. Axel thought it was an excellent idea, so he went off to fuel the boat and stow the canisters, and Hanna started packing a lunch.

Elis was very excited. He kept tapping the barometer for fear of storms and asking about the lighthouses on their islands – were they on real islands, tiny islands?

"Real fly specks," said Tom. "Why?"

Elis answered solemnly that he'd once read a story called "The Isle of Bliss" where the island had been very small.

"Yeah, yeah," said Tom. "Hurry up; Dad's waiting."

"Come on, jump in!" Axel cried. "We're off on a holiday, leaving all of our troubles behind!"

The children jumped aboard. Hanna stood on the dock and waved as the boat set off straight out to sea. It was a mild day, dazzlingly bright with high cumulus clouds mirrored in the sea and no horizon visible. Elis clung to the rail and watched for islands, occasionally turning to grin at Tom; he actually looked as if he was enjoying himself for once. So you're on holiday, you little shit, Tom thought. For the moment you've forgotten that the world's about to end, and you're only thinking of yourself. A bitter sense of injustice welled up in him and he decided to be totally indifferent to Elis all the way out and back again.

The first lighthouse had been built on a very low skerry with a windswept crest of low bushes in the middle. When they landed, gulls rose and circled, screaming. Axel heaved the fresh canisters ashore and dragged them up over the rocks to the lighthouse.

At first Elis just stood and stared, stiff as a poker, then he dashed off, rushed up into the brushwood, and flung himself back down again. Eider hens flew up from their nests with a great roar, but Elis hardly noticed. He ran back and forth shouting at the top of his lungs and finally threw himself headlong into a crowberry bush.

"I told you he's crazy," said Oswald scornfully. "And you let someone like that run after you all day and night. That's a fine friend you've made!"

Tom walked slowly up to where Elis was lying looking up at the sky, shamelessly contented.

Elis said, "I've never been on a real island before, one that looks like an island. It's so small it could be mine."

"You're babbling," Tom said. "Anyway, it belongs to the eiders too." Then he walked away.

When Axel came back ready to move on to the next lighthouse, Elis wouldn't budge. "I want to stay here," he said. "I like this island."

"But it could take a couple of hours," Axel objected. "We have to get to some lights a long way out. Much more interesting places, high ground, all kinds of things you'd like."

"It's okay," said Elis. "You go. I'll stay here."

They couldn't get him to change his mind. In the end, Axel took Tom aside and said, "You'd better stay here with him till I come back and pick you up. He might fall in the water or do something stupid, and we're responsible for the boy."

Little Mia was shouting, "Want to go to the next lighthouse! Want to go to the next lighthouse!"

"But Dad," said Tom, "I could be with him for hours on this tiny pancake of a place!"

"Course you could," said his father, pushing off. "Sometimes we all have to do things we don't like."

"Try and find him some old rotting birds!" Oswald shrieked across the water. "Babysitter!"

It wasn't till they reached the next lighthouse that Axel realised he still had the lunchbag with him. Hanna would never have done a thing like that, forgotten – but never mind, it could have been worse.

Then an hour later it did get worse. The fuel line broke, and you can't fix a thing like that with a flick of the wrist.

* * *

"You know what," said Elis, sounding almost reverent, "This island's wonderful. It's so far away, nothing dangerous can get to it. And the water's absolutely pure."

"That's what you think," Tom said. He went farther out on the headland and began throwing small stones in the water. There was absolutely nothing to do but wait and let the time go by and be totally bored. Ha ha, some "Isle of Bliss"! Dark thoughts came and went and came back again: a whole summer of endless torture and responsibility, not a chance of ever being really alone, surrounded by a bunch of stupid burials and rubbish heaps... And, as if today's misery wasn't bad enough, he'd get to hear about tomorrow's, when everything in the world would only get worse and worse. It wasn't fair!

And here came Elis running up with eyes out on stalks, shouting: "An island forgotten in the deep blue sea! It's fantastic! It's so clean! So desolate and deserted!"

"Fantastic, my foot," said Tom. "And it's not exactly deserted, with so many eider chicks hatching this year." He shrugged his shoulders and added, "Though there won't be so many broods, the way you carry on."

"What do you mean?"

"Just that if you scare an eider hen off her nest, she won't come back. They're very sensitive birds."

Elis said nothing. It was fun watching him stride deeper into the crowberry thicket, one slow step at a time with his elbows tight against his sides and his thin neck stretched forward. Now, by God, he could feel for himself what it's like to have someone give you a bad conscience. Tom followed him. Elis was staring down at five chicks, very small, dark and fluffy, sitting in their nest stock-still.

"Are they all right?" Elis whispered.

"Oh, don't think about it. Think about how you're on 'an island forgotten in the deep blue sea', isn't that what you said? It might interest you to know that a little island like this can get forgotten for real. It's hard to find your way back."

Elis just stared.

"Don't you believe me? It happens." Tom sat down and rested his chin in his hand. "I don't want to scare you, but sometimes they find human skeletons on beaches around here. Best not to think about it. They probably just sat there waiting and waiting and no one ever came."

"But he's got a map with him," Elis said.

"Does he? Come to think of it, he left the charts at home... and that could be bad." Tom sighed and glanced quickly at Elis through his fingers. He had a violent urge to giggle. How's this for one of your catastrophes? And I can make it worse. You wait and see.

Elis went and sat down behind a rock. The sun wandered on toward afternoon, the blackflies sang, and the seabirds quietly returned to their nests.

When Tom got hungry, he had a good idea. He went to Elis and told him they had a problem. They had nothing to eat – just like all those poor people all over the world. "Of course, you can eat crowberries," he said. "But they can give you a really bad stomachache. And, if you're thirsty there's a rock pool right behind you, although the water's so salty and stagnant that even the water lice have died." He decided to improve on this. "You can strain off their dead bodies through your teeth," he said, but he knew at once he was overdoing it, getting too personal, losing his touch. Elis gave him a long, sharp look and turned away.

The sea-water was taking on a deeper tone. The hours passed; Axel should have been back long ago. And there was nothing to do but scare Elis. Why had Axel not come? What did he mean by making him uneasy and wasting his whole day this way? It was starting to feel ominous, and he didn't like it.

"Elis!" he yelled. "Where are you? Come here a minute!"

Elis came and looked at him furtively.

"Listen," said Tom, "there's something I should tell you. This weather's not normal. There's a storm coming up."

"It's absolutely calm," said Elis, distrustful.

"The eye of the storm," Tom explained. "You know nothing about the sea. It can happen suddenly – bang. Waves can sweep over the whole island."

"But what about the lighthouse?"

"It's locked. We can't get in." Tom couldn't stop. "And snakes come out at night…"

"You're making it up."

"Maybe I am, and maybe I'm not. What are you going to do?"

Elis said slowly, "You don't like me."

* * *

The worst part of all was having nothing to do. Tom took out his sheath knife and went in among the windfalls to cut some twigs for a hut like the ones he used to build for Oswald when they went on expeditions. He whittled and worked until sweat ran down his neck, and it was all completely pointless, but he couldn't stand Elis looking at him all the time, and it was getting on towards evening and still no boat… And now Elis wanted to know if he was making a distress signal.

"No! Anyway we don't have any matches." Tom lifted the roof section of his hut and anchored it in the thicket. It was totally stupid, the whole thing was stupid, and still no boat… If there was a problem with one of the beacons – no, in that case he would have turned back right away. It must be something else, something serious… And then the whole roof section collapsed and he swung round on Elis, shouting, "How do you know what it's like when a storm comes up? You've never been in a storm! Everything goes dark… And you hear a strange sound coming closer and closer – and all the birds go all quiet…"

This was clearly making an impression, so he went on. "Sometimes before a storm the water level rises, but sometimes it falls. Catastrophically! You can see how low it is! Nothing but green slime everywhere. Then the waves come in like a wall and everything gets swept away – everything!"

"Why are you doing this?" Elis whispered.

"What do you mean?"

"Why don't you like me?"

"Well, why do you go on and on at me? I'm sick and tired of all of this; it's no fun any more! Go and find somewhere to sleep."

"But what about the snakes? I'm scared!"

"Oh all right, there aren't any snakes," Tom burst out impatiently. "There aren't ever any snakes on these little skerries. I'm worn out! I've tried, I've tried everything I can think of, but you just don't get any better. All you do is say weird stuff and you're making me almost as weird as you are. And Dad hasn't come, and he should have been here a long time ago!"

"I'm scared," said Elis again. "Do something... you know how to do stuff!" Suddenly he grabbed hold of Tom's shirt and kept whining on about how scared he was. "You scared me," he shouted. "Do something. You know how to do everything!"

Tom tore himself free so violently that Elis was thrown backwards. He sat there on the moss staring. His big eyes had shrunk to slits and he said slowly in a very low voice, "Yes, absolutely, your father should have been here a long time ago. Why hasn't he come? I'm sure it's not because he can't find us. You only said that to scare me. Something's happened to him."

Elis waited a moment and then went on triumphantly, "Perhaps he's broken his leg and he's just lying there. And we'll wait and wait, but he'll never come..."

"Bull!" said Tom, in a rage. "That sort of thing only happens in winter, when there's ice on the rocks." Then he suddenly remembered the time they sat waiting last autumn when Dad went out to the lighthouses with Oswald and the gas caught fire and shattered a lens right in his face, half blinding him, and he got them home as best he could, getting directions from Oswald, who just cried and cried...

Elis went on talking, never taking his eyes off Tom's face. "They don't know anything back home. It gets to be late. Finally they realise that something's happened. Does that sound right?"

"I say you're a sissy!" Tom yelled. "You're scared! You're so scared I can smell it..."

Suddenly, with incredible speed, Elis leaped to his feet and threw himself at Tom, who only had time to see two flashing rows of small teeth behind a desperate grimace before he was hurled to the ground in a grip that was bone-hard and blind with fury. They rolled in under the evergreen thicket where the light had almost gone, and fought under a low ceiling of tangled branches – you damned summer child, you little bastard, if you let go I don't know what I'll do to you, I'll hit you and keep hitting you. The skinny bony body under him seemed tense to the point of bursting; it was clear that defeat was impossible, unthinkable for either one of them. They had to keep going. They fought in total silence, soundlessly, breathlessly. Tom threw Elis aside and they separated, but they couldn't get up because there was no room under the branches, so they crawled back together and went on fighting, it was all they could do.

The eider hen sat quite still on her nest; she was the same colour as the ground. She did not move even when they caught sight of her and when they very carefully crept out from under the tangle of branches and went off in different directions.

Now it was night. The western sky was still burning like a rose down at the horizon, but it was definitely night. Tom walked down toward the beach where Axel usually came ashore. His whole body was shaking wildly and he was trying not to think, not think about anything. Let it be peaceful, please, let it be peaceful. All he wanted was to sit on the slope with his clenched fists pressed hard against his eyes and let it be peaceful. After a long time, a memory burst through and he let it come and it came. It was about the time the gas had exploded in the lighthouse. Mum asked, "Axel, what did you do?" Dad said, "I crawled for a bit till I could see again a little and got Oswald into the boat and tried to calm him down. At least there was no wind and that was good. You have to take things as they come." That's what he said – you have to take things as they come. And then I said, "Dad can get through anything and he's never scared." And Dad said, "You're wrong. I was never so scared in my life." That's just what he said – I was never so scared in my life.

Now came the midnight hour when the light in the western sky gives over to the dawn breaking from the other side. It was horribly cold. When Tom walked back in the half-light he could just make out Elis silhouetted against the sea, so he said, "He'll be coming now. He's been busy with something important, something he couldn't put off."

"You don't say," Elis said.

"I do say. And there's no wind and that's good. You have to take things as they come."

They stood a moment looking out to sea. Some gulls flew up from the headland and screamed for a while, and then it was quiet again.

Tom said, "Why don't you get some sleep? I'll wake you when he comes."

* * *

Axel came back at daybreak. First they heard the motor like a weak pulse, then it grew stronger, then the boat appeared as a little black speck on the grey morning sea and then they could see the white moustaches thrown up by the bow. Axel rounded the reef, reduced speed, and landed. He saw them standing there waiting and he knew at once. One had an improbably swollen and completely altered nose; the other could barely see out of one eye. Moreover, their clothes were torn.

"Well, well," said Axel. "So everything seems to be under control. Engine trouble, broken fuel line. I'm sorry about that, but you have to take things as they come. Everything okay?"

"Fine," said Elis.

"Come on, then. Jump in and we'll get home. But don't wake the kids, they're tired."

They sat down near the engine cover, where it was warmer, and Axel covered them with a tarp.

"Here's the lunchbag," said Axel. "Finish the lot or Hanna will be cross. There's coffee in the Thermos."

As the boat crossed the bay the sky in the east lightened and turned pink, and the first tiny glowing shard of the new sun appeared over the horizon. It was cold.

"Don't go to sleep just yet," said Axel. "I've got something for Elis that he's going to like. Look. Have you ever seen such a beautiful bird skeleton? You can bury it with pomp and circumstance."

"It's unusually pretty," said Elis. "And it was very kind of you to bring it to me, but I'm sorry to say I don't think I want it."

And he curled up next to Tom on the floor of the boat and they both fell instantly asleep.

A Foreign City

MY GRANDSON AND HIS WIFE had long been trying to persuade me to go south and pay them a visit. "You need to get away from the cold and the dark," they said, "and the sooner the better." Meaning: before it's too late.

I don't particularly like travelling, but I thought it best to accept their friendly offer and get it done. Moreover, they wanted to show off a daughter who'd come into the world a month or so earlier. No, maybe it was a year earlier. Whatever. They explained that the long flight would be too strenuous for me. They thought I should break the journey somewhere, spend the night in a comfortable hotel and continue the next day. Unnecessary. But I let them make the arrangements.

It was already dark when we landed for my stopover.

In the arrival lounge I realised I'd left my hat on the plane and tried to go back but they wouldn't let me through passport control. My legs hurt; I'd been sitting still for too long. I drew a hat on the cover of my ticket but they didn't understand and just waved me on to the

next window, where I handed over all the papers my
well-organised son had given me. Most had already been
checked and stamped but I showed them all again to
be on the safe side. I was disconcerted by this business
about my hat, and in any case I hate flying. It gradually
got through to me that they wanted to know how much
money I had with me, so I pulled out my wallet and let
them count it for themselves, then found some more in
my pockets. The whole thing took a terribly long time,
and by the time it was over nearly all the other passengers had vanished and I was afraid of missing the bus into
town. They motioned me to another window, where I'd
clearly already been. By now I was nervous and may have
seemed impatient. Whatever the reason, they took me
behind a counter and went through my suitcase. I had
no way of explaining to them that I was only nervous
because of my missing hat and my fear of missing the bus.
Yes, and my insurmountable hatred of flying – well, I've
already mentioned that.

Finally I drew another picture of a hat, lots of hats,
pointed to my head and tried to smile. They called over
an elderly man who seemed very calm. He looked at me
and my drawings and said something that might have
been, "Don't you understand? This gentleman has lost
his hat." At last I had the feeling I'd been understood
and wasn't the least bit surprised when they directed
me to the next window, where there was a little room
full of hats, gloves, umbrellas and the like. I took out
my drawing and, to make things clearer, shaded in the
hat with black. By now all the passengers had gone and

they'd begun turning off the lights in the arrivals hall; the luggage trolleys had been rolled away and I realised they wanted to be rid of me. I pointed at a hat up on a shelf and thumped the floor with my stick. They gave me the hat; it wasn't mine but I was so tired of the whole business I just put it on my head and signed a form. Of course, I wrote on the wrong line and had to do it all over again.

When I finally got out of the building, the road was empty. The formless desolation so characteristic of airport surroundings stretched away on all sides. The night was cold and misty. When I listened I could hear the city far away and had an impression of absolute unreality. But I said to myself, this is absolutely no cause for alarm, this is simply an unfortunate situation that is never likely happen again. Calm down. Just wait. For a while I thought about going back and asking someone to ring me a taxi. "Taxi" must be more or less the same in all languages, and of course I could always draw a little car. But somehow I didn't feel like going back into the dark arrivals hall. Perhaps the last plane had taken off and there were no more due to arrive that night; what did I know about their big – well, their flying machines as we called them when I was young! My legs hurt and I was very vexed. The road seemed endless, with long dark spaces between the street lamps. I remembered that they were short of electricity.

So I waited. I began tormenting myself again with the fact that my memory is getting worse, an annoying insight that often afflicts me whenever I have to wait. And I can't help noticing that I often repeat myself, say the same things to the same person several times and realise it only afterwards, always with a sense of shame. And words disappear as easily as hats, as easily as faces and names.

As I stood there waiting for a taxi, a terrible realisation began to dawn on me. At first I pushed it aside, but it wouldn't go away, and in the end I was forced to face the disagreeable fact that I'd forgotten the name of my hotel. Completely. I took out my papers and went through them all. Nothing. I spread them out on my suitcase under a streetlamp and got down on my knees so as not to miss the tiniest little scribbled note. I searched my pockets yet again. Nothing. Back home, my methodical son must have given me some sort of confirmation that the hotel had been paid for, but where had I left it – somewhere in the arrivals lounge or back on the plane? No. I'd have to remember. But the harder I cudgelled my brain for the name of the hotel, the emptier it became. And I knew it was impossible to get a hotel room in this city unless you'd booked it far in advance.

Now I was afraid to get a taxi. I began sweating and took off the hat, which was in any case too small and pinched my head. And then, as I stood there in the uncertain light of the street lamp with this strange hat in my hand, I noticed there was a name in it; the owner had written his name in the hat. I put on my glasses; yes, unquestionably a name and an address. It was a comfort, a foothold. A genuine communication. I tried to shake off my fatigue. When I get tired, everything slips away from me. I want to be attentive, aware, decisive, not slow down and lose my way. And not repeat myself. People notice that immediately; they become polite and embarrassingly sympathetic. I know at once when I've been repeating myself. Unfortunately, just the tiniest bit too late... But I've already said that.

And now here came a taxi, at first far away down the long road, then nearer, headlights dimmed, it drew up and stopped in front of me. What could have been more natural than to show the driver the address in the hat? Without a word he began driving towards the city. I let my thoughts rest. It was a long way; the buildings around us were dark, and if anything the mist had grown thicker. When the car stopped I took out my wallet while he sat still, his taxi meter switched off. "Dollars," he said finally. I handed them to him, one after another. It was quite impossible to tell when the man had received enough, he just lifted his shoulders and looked straight ahead. Rest assured that by the time I finally got out of the car with my suitcase, I was thoroughly sick and tired of the whole journey. The house in front of me was very old; it looked medieval. The square was totally deserted.

I opened the front door and only then realised how lucky I was; it could so easily have been locked. Stairs and high corridors, numbers on the doors but no names. I changed into my strongest glasses, the ones I use for stamp collecting, and read what was written in the hat. It is so reassuring that there are people in the world who still take the trouble to write out a long address in clear handwriting. Number twelve, it said. I knocked and the door opened immediately.

Somehow I'd expected an older man – I mean, someone who might be expected to forget a hat, but this man was very young, tall and strongly built with a mass of shiny black hair. Of course, I ought to have learned at least a couple of phrases: good evening, excuse me, I'm so sorry but I don't speak your language... As it was, I just held the hat out to him and said, "Sorry". He hesitated, perhaps thinking I expected him to put something in the hat, so I quickly turned it crown upwards and said "Sorry" again.

At that he smiled and said in English, "Can I help you?"

My relief was enormous.

"I think this is your hat," I said. "I'm terribly sorry, I'm afraid I took it by mistake... Look, this is your name and address, isn't it?"

He looked and said, "Remarkable. This hat belongs to my cousin. He was living here six months ago. Where did you find it?"

"On the plane."

"Of course. He gets to fly sometimes. He's a civil servant. Come in, it's cold this evening. It was kind of you to go to so much trouble so late at night."

The room was a small one. In the light from the single table lamp I got a general impression of pleasant homely untidiness: books, newspapers and piles of papers all over the place. It was very cold.

He asked me where I was from and did I know the city... Oh, of course, just passing through. But it was unusual for people to break their journey here. Unless they had business here, of course. Would I care for a cup of tea?

I watched him lift the kettle from the stove and take out cups. All his movements were very calm. Occasionally he looked at me and smiled. It was so peaceful to be able to sit with him and drink tea and quietly wait for the name of my hotel to pop up. I was dreadfully tired. After his first polite questions, he said nothing more, but it was a pleasant silence.

In the end I remarked on the fact that he had so many books. And on how it was difficult these days to get your hands on the books you wanted.

"Yes. It is very difficult. People keep track of what's being published and, when it comes out, somehow they know, they sniff it out. And go and queue for it. I'm very proud of my library."

"You're a writer, perhaps?"

"Not really. Just articles, in a way."

"And what kind of books particularly interest you?"

He smiled again and said, "Everything."

I said that I myself, on a modest scale, had published a bit on the subject of, how should I put it, the changes that affect us as we get older. I wondered if I could send him a couple of books.

"Please do. They might reach me. The post isn't always reliable."

Then it was time for me to go. It was terribly late. My suitcase was waiting by the door. A taxi, of course. But I couldn't see a telephone. He watched me looking round the room and said, "No, I have no phone. But I can go out and try and find you a taxi. It's not so difficult, but it may take some time." He got up. When he reached the door I called out, "One moment... I'm extremely sorry, this is really embarrassing." In my shame I tried to be funny. "A propos the changes caused by ageing... I, if anyone, should be able to explain how a person can forget the name of the hotel where he's booked a room."

My host did not seem amused, nor did he attempt to make light of it. He stood and thought for a while, then explained that, since it was impossible to find hotel rooms in the city, it would be best if I spent the night with him. Somehow it seemed unnecessary to raise polite objections. He explained that sometimes as many as half a dozen people spent the night in his apartment. He pulled out a sleeping bag and promised to wake me in good time for my flight. I was to have his bed; I accepted.

There was a knock on the door. Luckily I had not yet started undressing. It was a young woman with dark hair. She glanced at me almost without interest, walked past him to the window, carefully drew aside the curtain and looked out. They began talking together, very rapidly. Even though I couldn't understand, I grasped that something serious had happened. He started walking back and forth across the room, opening drawers, taking out papers, glancing through them quickly before shoving them into a paper bag. He was clearly in a hurry, but his movements remained as calm as ever. Finally he turned to me and said, "I'm afraid I have to go. But please stay and sleep in peace; my friend will come and wake you in good time for your flight. Don't forget to send me the books; I'd be very happy to get them."

I just nodded. I didn't want to delay him. When they had gone I listened carefully and heard them go down the stairs, heard the front door close. I continued listening. By now they must have crossed the square and made it into the streets beyond. I lay down on the bed but couldn't fall asleep.

About half an hour later, there was a pounding on the door. Someone shouted God knows what, and I got up and let them in. By now I was so tired I noticed only a number of uniforms filling the room. I had to show my passport and my tickets. They stripped everything they could out of the drawers and cupboards, while a single thought repeated itself in my head: he got away, my friend got away.

In the morning the young woman came and woke me in good time. She had found a taxi and came with me to the airport. She got very angry with the driver – I think because he was demanding dollars. I hadn't even learned to say thank you, but I believe she understood.

As I say, I often repeat myself, but this story has never been told before. At least, I don't think so.

The Woman Who
Borrowed Memories

THE STAIRWELL WITH ITS STAINED-GLASS windows was as dark and cold as it had been fifteen years earlier. Some of the plaster ornamentation had fallen off the ceiling. And like fifteen years ago, Mrs Lundblad was busy scrubbing the stairs. She looked up at the sound of the door and exclaimed in delight, "Well, I'll be! If it isn't Miss Stella! Abroad for so long! And just like the old days – trench coat and no hat!"

Stella ran up the stairs and stopped almost shyly in front of Mrs Lundblad; they had known each other well, but had never been in the habit of hugging or shaking hands.

"Nothing's changed here!" said Stella. "Dear Mrs Lundblad, how's your family? Charlotta? Edvin?"

Mrs Lundblad pushed aside her bucket and said that Charlotta was still enjoying Stella's bicycle, although these days only in the country; they now rented a little summer cottage. And Edvin had a good job with an insurance company.

"And Mr Lundblad?"

"Passed away six years ago," said Mrs Lundblad. "Peacefully; he didn't suffer much. I see you have flowers with you, Miss. I expect they're for her, upstairs in your old studio. Have you time for a cigarette?" She sat down on the stairs. "I see we both still smoke the same brand. And now you've gone and got famous for your paintings! We've read all about it in the paper, so congratulations from the whole family. Are your pictures still the same?"

Stella laughed. "Oh no! They're so big these days, they wouldn't even fit through the door up there! As big as this!" She stretched out her arms.

A blast of loud dance music suddenly filled the stairwell and was almost instantly switched off again. Stella recognised it: "Evening Blues". That used to be our tune, she thought, Sebastian's and mine. So she's still got my old 78s...

"She does that all the time," said Mrs Lundblad, tossing her cigarette butt into her pail. "Five years older than you, Miss, and still living her life as if it's a nonstop party; not that anyone ever comes to see her. The place is empty. Not like when you used to live up there! All those artists running up the stairs – it was fun. They'd work all day and come here in the evening and play and sing and you'd make them all spaghetti. Remember, Miss? And she'd hang around trying to be like the rest of you?" Mrs Lundblad lowered her voice. "And then you let her stay there for ages when she couldn't pay her rent, for heaven's sake, and then you won that scholarship and went abroad and she just took the whole place. Fifteen years! No, no, don't say a word. I know what I know. Any idea, Miss, what we used to call the studio? The swallows' nest! But all the swallows flew away. And it's like that old saying: when the swallows go, it's because the home's no longer a happy one. And one swallow doesn't make a summer. Now, enough's enough. I'm not saying another word. I'll just get on with these stairs. Oh, and they've put in a new lift at the back. Would you like to try it?"

"Maybe not today. Tell me, Mrs Lundblad, did I really use to run up all these stairs?"

"Yes, Miss, you surely did. But time passes."

There were lots of unfamiliar names on the doors of the flats.

Well of course I ran. Maybe just because I liked to run. I couldn't help it.

The studio door had been repainted but the knocker with its little brass lion was the same, a present from Sebastian. Wanda called from inside, "Who is it? Is that you, Stella?"

"Yes it's me. It's Stella."

A moment passed before the door opened.

"Darling, how wonderful," cried Wanda. "You're finally here, imagine! It takes a bit of time to open the door, but you know how it is these days: one can't be too careful... Safety chain, police lock, everything... But there's no choice, there's just no choice – they steal! One has to be careful day and night; they come in vans and take everything and just drive off... They clean you out, you know, just leave the place empty! But not here! This door's locked and bolted. But come in and have a look around! Flowers – how nice of you..." She set the flowers aside still wrapped and inspected Stella intently with the same pale, fixed gaze, unchanged in a somewhat heavier face. And the same insistent voice. The walls were still whitewashed, but everything else in the very small room was new and different: an excess of furniture, lamps, ornaments, draperies... It was much too warm. Stella took off her coat. The room was shrunken and frightening. As if trees had been cut and a thicket of undergrowth had taken their place.

"But make yourself comfortable," Wanda said. "What can I get you? Vermouth? Or wine? Like I used to serve in the old days, red wine and spaghetti! Always red wine and spaghetti! So you've finally come back. How many years has it been – no, we won't count them. Anyway, now you're here. And all those cards I wrote, and you just disappeared; the great artist vanishes into a great silence. That's life!"

"But I did write to you," Stella put in. "For a long time. But when I heard nothing from you..."

"Stella, dear, don't worry about it, don't even think about it, let's just forget it. Now you're here again. What do you think of my little lair? Small and unpretentious, but pleasant, don't you think? Lots of atmosphere."

"Very nice. Such nice furniture." Stella closed her eyes and tried to remember the studio the way it had been – workbench here, easel there, lots of wooden boxes... And a bare window overlooking the courtyard.

"Are you maybe a bit tired?" said Wanda. "You look exhausted. Around the eyes. Now you can rest a little and take it easy after the big wide world."

Stella said, "I was just trying to remember the studio. We were so happy here. Imagine, seven years of our youth! Wanda, how long do you think we get to be young?"

Wanda answered quite sharply, "You were young for too long. Starry-Eyes. Yes, that's what we called you, Starry-Eyes. Nice, isn't it? So naive, you believed everything anyone told you. Everything."

Stella stood up and went to the window. She pulled the drapes aside and looked out over the grey, very ordinary, still fascinating courtyard with all its windows and remembered: I stood here with Sebastian. We looked out beyond the roofs, out over the harbour, out over the sea, out over the whole world that we were going to own, battle our way through and conquer. This very window! She turned to face Wanda. "You said I believed whatever people told me. But there was so much to believe in, wasn't there? And it was well worth it, don't you think?"

Dusk was falling and Wanda switched on the lights behind their silk shades. She said, "You had fun in this room, didn't you? You had fun for seven years, right up to the last party, my farewell party. Do you remember?"

"Do I remember! Great speeches, we were so profound! It was June, I think, with the sun coming up at two in the morning. And I stood on the table and shouted, 'Skoal to the sun!' And there was a Russian sitting under the table singing. Where did he come from?"

"The Russian? I think he was one of those people we always included because we felt sorry for them. And there were a lot of those, way too many! But I always let them come. 'Bring them along,' I'd say. 'The more the merrier.' That's my principle. If you're having a party, then do it in style! We got twenty-two people in here, twenty-two. I counted. One of the best parties I've ever given for my friends."

"What do you mean?" Stella said. "It was my party!"

"Yes, yes, of course, if you like. I gave a farewell party for you, so of course, in a sense, it was your party. Then off you went on the morning train."

Yes, the morning train, Stella thought. Sebastian came with me to the train. A lovely summer morning... He promised he'd follow as soon as he'd sorted out his travel grant, as soon as I'd found us a studio, or a room, or a cheap hotel, anywhere we could work... He hardly ever had a fixed address, so I was to send the address to Wanda... Bye-bye, darling, take care of yourself! And the train whistled and rushed out into the world.

"Now, don't go upsetting yourself about my party, Stella. Though surely you haven't forgotten that I was the one who lived here. This was my home. Be honest, it was my place, wasn't it? Of course it was." Wanda laid her hand over Stella's and went on in a friendly voice. "Memory plays funny tricks. But don't worry about it; it's totally natural. You're every bit as welcome now as you were then. You were such a great help; you helped in so many ways, peeling onions and carrying out the garbage... And we included you in everything, our poor little Starry-Eyes... Wait a second, there's the lift..."

The sound of the lift was very loud.

"Third floor," said Wanda. "Funny how often it goes to the third floor. Yes, all the things we did back then, and now here you sit in your old spot, between Ingegerd and Tommi and me on the sofa, with Bennu opposite. Sebastian used to sit in the window. You all talked and talked about art – all you cared about was your work. And how many of you became famous, can you tell me that?"

"It's so easy to lose track of how your friends got on," Stella said.

"You don't know? Did none of them ever write to you? But Stella, sweetheart!"

Stella lit a cigarette. "I sent you my address and asked you to pass it on to my friends."

"Did you? Hang on, your cigarette's not lit. Here, this is a good lighter. You should start using a lighter; your hands have started to shake, just a little, just a tiny bit, nothing to worry about. Whatever. Well, Sebastian became quite famous, in a way. But you know how it is with great men; they forget the people who believed in them when they were a bit less great. Aren't you going to finish your wine?"

Stella said, "Do you know how he is? Do you know where he is?"

They heard the lift again and sat quietly.

"Fourth floor," remarked Wanda. "Time to put on the spaghetti, I think. *Al burro*. With Parmesan these days! You like Parmesan?"

"Yes, thanks. Are you still at the council offices?"

"Certainly am, and looking forward to my pension like everyone else. I'm departmental manager now."

"Really? What do you do with the rest of your time? Same hobby? Still doing your gymnastics in the evenings?"

"In the evenings? You're mad. One doesn't dare go out on the streets after six o'clock in this city!" Wanda went to the little kitchen in the corner to put the water on to boil. She set the table.

"Would you like to see Jaska's photographs?"

It was a beautiful album full of bad photographs of a tight crowd of laughing young people – at a fancy-dress party, at the beach in a strong wind, on their way somewhere carrying easels – charming snapshots of no interest whatsoever except to those who were there at the time.

Stella said, "This was at Hanaholmen. I was standing beside Sebastian in my white dress. You can still see a bit of that dress."

Wanda looked and said, "That wasn't you, that was someone else. Light got in, so I had to cut off one corner. Do you use ketchup?"

"No, I don't. Do you know where Sebastian is now?"

"I might. But the thing is, dear, it's a secret. I promised not to give the address to anyone. Say what you like about me, I'm loyal to my friends. And anyway, it wasn't Hanaholmen, it was Äggskär. And you weren't even there that time. Memory's funny, isn't it? Some things just disappear and others you never forget. Are memories important to you? Be frank, think about it. Those days when everything was so easy for you. This room. You'd like to go back, wouldn't you?"

"Not any more," said Stella. "I think the water's boiling."

But the water wasn't boiling; the gas tokens had run out.

"I'm so sorry," said Wanda. "Forgive me. I could go down and borrow some from Mrs Lundblad, but she's so unpleasant..."

"Never mind. She's probably busy with the stairs."

"You saw her? What did she say?"

"Well, we talked a bit about this and that."

"But what did she say about me?"

"Nothing."

"Are you sure?"

"Absolutely. She didn't say a thing. It's really hot in here, Wanda. Do you think we could open the window for a bit?"

The spring evening came into the room, cool and liberating.

"This window," said Wanda. "I remember you standing here laughing, you and Sebastian. You were laughing at the rest of us, weren't you? What was so funny? Who were you laughing at?"

Wanda's voice, flat, insistent and inescapable, was suddenly too much for Stella, and she lost her temper. "We weren't laughing at anyone! Or we were laughing at all of you, at everything! Because we were happy! We looked at each other and laughed; it was fun. Is that so hard to understand?"

"But why are you so angry?" said Wanda, distressed.

"I'm tired. You talk too much."

"Do I? Silly me, so thoughtless. And I can see you're not feeling well. You've changed so much. Is something wrong? You can tell me. Stella. Come and sit here on the sofa. Did those photos upset you? They're just innocent old memories for safekeeping."

"You're right – they're innocent. This studio was innocent in those days too. It was a place where everything was friendly and straightforward. We worked and we trusted each other, because everything was open and above board. I think about this place when I'm having trouble getting to sleep."

"Trouble sleeping? That's not good. Not good at all. Listen, Stella, you're not yourself. Have you seen a doctor? I mean, this business of forgetting things... But that's probably not so serious, nothing to worry about."

"The lift!" Stella yelled. "There it goes again. Wait till it stops!"

"That was the fourth floor."

Wanda closed the window and filled their glasses. She was still talking. "He bought me a record even though they cost a fortune. And the other artists would also bring me a record now and then. Little me... We used to dance. Till dawn. And you know what I'd do then? I'd get up on the table and drink a toast with all of you and shout, 'Skoal to the sun!' And when the party was over and everyone had gone home and there was only the two of us, Sebastian and me... Stella? How about a bit of music? An old 78 he gave me. 'Evening Blues'."

"No, not right now." Stella had a headache, a nasty pain behind her eyes. The lift started up again, almost right to the top. In this altered room she recognised only one thing: the bookcase. She reached out and touched it.

"I knocked that up in a single evening," Wanda said. "Pretty good, don't you think?"

Stella burst out, "That's not true! That's my old bookcase that I made with my own two hands!"

Wanda leaned back in her chair and smiled. "What a fuss about nothing! That old bookcase? Take it, it's yours, a present. But Stella, dear, I'm worried about you. Where did you lose your starry eyes? What's wrong, dear? Can't you tell me about it? And now another cigarette. You smoke too much. You don't look at all well. Take it easy, I beg you. Stop trying to remember the way things used to be; you just get sad and confused. That's it, isn't it? Tell me the truth. It makes you unhappy and confused. It was all so long ago now and, you know, the years haven't been kind to you. Anyway, what's so special about this old bookcase? Nothing. Think about something pleasant. Remember Tommi? He was nice, and he fancied you. He'd say, 'We have to look after our little Starry-Eyes. She's so docile, she swallows everything. She's our little rubbish bin: we fill her up and there's always room for more...'"

Stella broke in. "I don't think we should talk any more about those days. We could talk about what's happening now. Out there."

"What do you mean – out there?"

"Out in the world. The great upheavals, all the violent and important things going on everywhere all the time.

We could talk about that." She could see that Wanda didn't understand, so she added, "The stuff we read about in the papers."

"I don't get a paper," said Wanda. "Anyway, Tommi liked you. All my friends liked you. Believe me, it's true. And it absolutely wasn't pity…"

"That lift!" Stella burst out. "There it goes again!"

"So?"

"Are you expecting someone, or are you afraid?"

"Of what?"

"Burglars, Wanda, all the burglars who are going to come in and take your things!"

Wanda looked straight at her guest. "Don't be childish. No one can get in here." There was a moment's silence, then Wanda went on. "You remind me of someone, one of the ones we felt sorry for, who only came here to eat. She used to eat and eat and never say a word. Funny – she was like you. Poor thing. She used to follow me about everywhere. And you know what she said to me once: 'You're so strong,' she said. 'You're like a strong electric current. You make me move faster, you make me feel alive!' Then she disappeared. No one knew what happened to her and no one cared… Stella? What's the matter – don't you feel well?"

"No,' said Stella, "I don't feel well. Do you have an aspirin?"

"Of course, right away… But darling, lie down on the sofa for a bit. No, I insist. You look terrible, you need to lie down. Don't talk. Just promise me you'll go for a proper check-up soon; it's so easy to do."

Stella felt a great urge to sleep; the room disappeared. The inescapable voice whispered on, "Are you comfortable? Here in this room you're with me and you can forget and let go... All of them, they all come to my room, they stand waiting at the door and I hear them and let them in and they talk and talk... Worries, worries, worries... Then I talk, frankly and honestly. One has to be completely honest, doesn't one? Don't you agree? One needn't say so very much, but one has to weigh one's words, one must find just the right words; it's so important. But you're freezing! Hang on, let me tuck you up nice and cosy... No, no, let me look after you – I'm right, aren't I, about daring to be honest?"

Stella screamed, "Let me go!" But the blanket crept up over her face and the voice droned on: "I told him what I thought, what I honestly thought. I said, 'She's suffocating you, you have to get rid of her...'"

"The lift!" Stella screamed, and for a moment the grip loosened. She jumped to her feet and ran to the middle of the room. Wanda was left sitting on the sofa. "Stella? What are you looking for?"

"My bag, my bag!"

Wanda laughed. "Well, I didn't steal it! It has to be here somewhere. I locked the door from the inside. Sit down and relax. I'll tell you how things are. Have a little more wine. No? Listen, being at home in your own room, where everything belongs to you and it's all there, everything that's happened and everything that's been said, it's all there, the walls are steeped in it, it's all around you like a warm cloak and it holds you tighter and tighter...

Don't you believe me? I can prove it! I've got a recording. Please just listen and you'll understand."

There came an incomprehensible chaos of voices and shrill music. Wanda cried out, "You hear that? That proves it, doesn't it? There's a glass breaking – you hear that?"

Stella stood at the locked door holding her bag and coat. "Wanda, let me out! Let me go."

"No, don't go, please, don't go yet, stay a little longer, just a little while, it was all so long ago and there's still so much to talk about... What are you afraid of? It's not late, not at all, the streets aren't dangerous yet, not till later, but then you can take a taxi and I'll come down and make sure you get away all right... Stella? There's no need to worry, I mean if you've got a lot of money in your bag and you're scared of being robbed..."

"I've already been robbed," said Stella. "Just let me out."

Wanda came to the door and took her by the arm. "Stella? Is it the bookcase? Take it, please. I'd like you to have it! It's so small, you can take it in a taxi. Don't look at me like that, don't be mean to me..." Her hand was still on Stella's arm. Stella took it in her own and held it silently it until it was calm. Then Wanda unlocked the door and stood aside. Stella went down the stairs feeling wildly and inconsolably relieved. At the corner she turned to say goodbye but the door was already closed. "Evening Blues" began to play and then stopped again almost immediately.

A thick fog had descended over the city, the first spring fog. A good sign. It meant that soon, little by little, the ice would go.

Travelling Light

I WISH I COULD DESCRIBE the enormous relief I felt when they finally pulled up the gangway! Only then did I feel safe. Or, more exactly, when the ship had moved far enough from the quay for it to be impossible for anyone to call out... ask for my address, scream that something awful had happened... Believe me, you can't imagine my giddy sense of freedom. I unbuttoned my overcoat and took out my pipe but my hands were shaking and I couldn't light it; but I stuck it between my teeth anyway, because that somehow establishes a certain detachment from one's surroundings. I went as far forward as possible in the bows, from where it was impossible to see the city, and hung over the railing like the most carefree traveller you can imagine. The sky was light blue, the little clouds seemed whimsical, pleasantly capricious...

Everything was in the past now, gone, of no significance; nothing mattered any more, no one was important. No telephone, no letters, no doorbell. Of course you have no idea what I'm referring to, but it doesn't matter anyway; in fact I shall merely assert that everything had been sorted out to the best of my ability, thoroughly taken care of down to the smallest detail. I wrote the letters I had to write – in fact, I'd done that as long ago as the day before, announcing my sudden departure without explanation and without in any way accounting for my behaviour. It was very difficult; it took a whole day. Of course, I left no information about where I was going and indicated no time for my return, since I have no intention of ever coming back. The caretaker's wife will look after my houseplants; those tired living things – which never look well no matter how much trouble one takes over them – have made me feel very uneasy. Never mind: I shan't ever have to see them again.

Perhaps it might interest you to know what I packed? As little as possible! I've always dreamed of travelling light, a small weekend bag of the sort one can casually whisk along with oneself as one walks with rapid but unhurried steps through, shall we say, the departure lounge of an airport, passing a mass of nervous people dragging along large heavy cases. This was the first time I'd succeeded in taking the absolute minimum with me, ruthless in the face of family treasures and those little objects one can become so attached to that remind one of... well, of emotional bits of one's life – no, that least of all! My bag was as light as my happy-go-lucky heart and contained nothing more than one would need for a routine night at a hotel. I left the flat without leaving instructions of any kind, but I did clean it, very thoroughly. I'm very good at cleaning. Then I turned off the electricity, opened the fridge and unplugged the phone. That was the very last thing, the definitive step; now I'd done with them.

And during all this time the phone never rang once – a good omen. Not one, not a single one of all these, these – but I don't want to talk about them now, I'm not going to worry about them any more, no, they no longer occupy even a single second of my thoughts. Well, when I'd pulled out the phone plug and checked one last time that I had all the papers I needed in my pocketbook – passport, tickets, travellers' cheques, pension card – I looked out of the window to make sure that there were some taxis waiting at the stand on the corner, shut the front door and let the keys fall through the letterbox.

Out of old habit I avoided the lift; I don't like lifts. On the second floor I tripped and grabbed hold of the banisters, and stood still a moment, suddenly hot all over. Think, just think – what if I'd really fallen, maybe sprained my ankle or worse? Everything would have been in vain, fatal, irreparable. It would have been unthinkable to get ready and gather myself together to leave a second time. In the taxi I felt so exhilarated I carried on a lively conversation with the driver, commenting on the early spring weather and taking an interest in this and that relating to his profession, but he hardly responded at all. I pulled myself together, because this was exactly what I'd decided to avoid; from now on I was going to be a person who never took any interest in anyone. The problems that might face a taxi driver were nothing to do with me. We reached the boat much too early, he lifted out my bag, I thanked him and gave him too big a tip. He didn't smile, which upset me a bit, but the man who took my ticket was very friendly.

My journey had started. It gradually got cold on deck; there was hardly anyone else there and I presumed the other passengers must have made their way to the restaurant. Taking my time, I went to find my cabin. I saw at once that I wasn't going to be alone; someone had left a coat, pocketbook and umbrella on one of the bunks, and two elegant suitcases were standing in the middle of the floor. Discreetly, I moved them out of the way. Of course I had demanded, or more accurately expressed a desire to have, a cabin to myself; sleeping on my own has become very important to me and on this journey in particular it was absolutely essential for me to, so to speak, savour my new independence entirely undisturbed. I couldn't possibly go and complain to the purser, who would have merely pointed out that the boat was full, that it was a regrettable misunderstanding, and that if the misunderstanding were to be rectified I would be aware all night as I lay on my solitary bunk that the man who was to have shared my cabin was having to spend the night sleepless on a deckchair.

I noticed that his toilet articles were of exclusive quality, and I was particularly impressed by his light-blue electric toothbrush and a miniature case with the monogram A.C. on it. I unpacked my own toothbrush and the other things I had considered necessary from my ascetic point of view, laid out my pyjamas on the other bunk and asked myself if I was hungry. The thought of the likely crush in the restaurant put me off, so I decided to skip dinner and have a drink in the bar instead. The bar was pretty empty this early in the evening. I sat down on one of the high stools, propped my feet on the traditional metal railing which runs round every bar on the continent, and lit my pipe.

"A Black and White, please," I said to the bartender, accepting the glass with a brief nod and making clear with my attitude that I had no inclination for conversation. I sat and pondered the Idea of Travel; that is to say, the act of travelling unfettered and with no responsibility for what one has left behind and without any opportunity to foresee what may lie ahead and prepare for it. Nothing but an enormous sense of peace.

It occurred to me to think back over my earlier journeys, every one of them, and I realised to my astonishment that this must be the first time I had ever travelled alone. First came my trips with my mother – Majorca and the Canaries. Majorca again. After mother went away I travelled with Cousin Herman, to Lübeck and Hamburg. He was only interested in museums, though they depressed him; he'd never been able to study painting and he couldn't get over it. Not a happy trip. Then the Wahlströms, who didn't know whether to divorce or not and thought it would be easier to travel as a threesome.

Where did we go…? Oh, yes, of course, Venice. And during the mornings they quarrelled. No, that wasn't much of a journey. What next? A trip with a party to Leningrad. It was damn cold… And then Aunt Hilda, who needed a break but didn't dare go by herself... but that was only as far as Mariehamn; we went to the Maritime Museum there, I remember. You see, when I went through all my life's journeys in my thoughts, any fear I possibly could have had that the way I'd decided to do things might not be right disappeared. I turned to the bartender, said, "Another, please," and looked round the bar, very much at ease. People had started coming in; happy well-fed people who ordered coffee and drinks to their tables and crowded round me at the bar.

Normally I very much dislike crowds and do everything I can to avoid being involved with them, even in buses and trams, but that evening it felt pleasant and sociable to be one among many, almost secure. An elderly gentleman with a cigar intimated with a discreet gesture that he needed my ashtray. "Of course, don't mention it," I responded and was on the point of begging his pardon but remembered in time: I'd finished with all that kind of thing. In an entirely matter-of-fact way, if with a certain nonchalance, I moved the ashtray to his side and calmly studied myself in the mirror behind the bottles in the bar.

There's something special about a bar, don't you think? A place for chance happenings, for possibilities to become reality, a refuge on the awkward route from should to must. But, I must confess, not the sort of place I've much frequented. Now, as I sat and looked in the mirror, my face suddenly seemed rather agreeable.

I suppose I had never allowed myself time to look closely at the appearance time has given me. A thin face with somewhat surprised but frankly beautiful eyes, hair admittedly grey but luxuriant in an almost artistic manner, with a lock hanging down over my brow giving me an expression of – what shall we say – anxious watchfulness? Watchful concern? No. Just watchfulness. I emptied my glass and suddenly felt an urgent need to communicate, but held it in check. At all events, despite everything, wasn't this precisely an occasion when, at last, I would not be forced to listen but could be allowed to talk myself, freely and recklessly? Among men, in a bar? For example, entirely in passing of course, I might let slip information about my decisive contribution at the Post Office. But no. Absolutely not. Be secretive – don't make confidences; at most, drop hints...

Sitting on my left was a young man who seemed extremely restless. He kept moving his position, turning this way and that on his stool and seemingly trying to keep an eye on everything that was happening in the room. I turned to the neighbour on my other side and said, "Very crowded this evening. Looks like we're in for a calm crossing." He stubbed his cigar in the ashtray and remarked that the boat was full and that our wind speed was eight metres per second, though they'd forecast it would get stronger during the night. I liked his calm matter-of-fact manner and asked myself whether he was retired and why he should be on his way to London. Let me tell you, my interest surprised myself; nothing has become so completely foreign, almost hateful to me, to be avoided at all costs, as curiosity and sympathy, any disposition to encourage in the slightest degree the surrounding world's irresistible need to start talking about its troubles. This is something I really do know about; during a long life I've heard most things and I've brought this entirely on myself. But, as I've said, I was sitting in a bar on the way to my new freedom – and I was being a bit careless.

He said: "You're going to London? On business?"

"No. Sea travel amuses me."

He nodded in appreciation. I could see his face in the mirror, a rather heavy face somewhat the worse for wear with a drooping moustache and tired eyes. He seemed elegant, expensively dressed, continental, if you know what I mean.

"When I was young," he said, "I worked out that it should be possible to travel by sea all the time, without stopping, meals included, for very much less than it costs to live in a city."

I watched him, fascinated, waiting for him to go on, but he said nothing more. Thank goodness, this was clearly not a man to make personal confidences. Meanwhile, soft music was throbbing persistently somewhere up in the ceiling and people had begun talking with increasing animation, while trays heavily laden with glasses were being carried with impressive speed and precision between the tables. I thought: 'Here I am sitting with an experienced traveller, a man who has taken the best from life and knows what he's talking about.' It was then he took out his pocketbook and showed me pictures of his family and his dog. That was a warning signal. A sharp sense of disappointment pierced me – but why should I be surprised if my companion was showing signs of behaving exactly like all the others? But I'd decided not to let anything whatever upset me, so I looked at his snapshots and said all the usual nice things. His wife, children, grandchildren and dog looked more or less just as one would expect, except that they seemed in an unusually flourishing condition.

He sighed – of course, I couldn't hear him sigh in all that din, but I saw his broad shoulders rise and fall. Clearly not all was as it should be at home. I know; it's the same with them all. Even this most elegant, cigar-smoking traveller with his gold lighter and his family posing in front of his swimming pool – even him! I hurriedly began talking about the first thing that came into my head, the advantages of travelling light, and made up my mind to detach myself gradually from the man; I mean, get away as quickly as possible without seeming brusque. I dropped a hint by taking out my cabin key, laying it beside my glass and trying to catch the bartender's attention, naturally without success – the crush round the bar was worse than ever, increasingly impatient and loud, and the poor man was working like a maniac.

"Two Black and Whites," said my travel companion in a low voice but with the sort of calm, powerful authority that ensures immediate results. He fixed his heavy gaze on me and raised his glass. Now I was caught.

"Thanks," I said. "How nice – a little nightcap. It's getting quite late, I think."

He answered, "Not at all, Mr Melander. My name's Connaugh." And he laid his cabin key beside mine. "An incredible coincidence," I exclaimed, most put out.

"Oh no. I saw you coming out of the cabin. Your bag's very neatly labelled."

Suddenly I was jostled by the young man on my left as he leaned aggressively forward across the bar to demand a Cuba Libre. He'd now had to ask three times but, no, everyone else must come first. Typical, just what you'd expect... Mr Connaugh gave the youngster a very brief and very cold glance and said, "It seems to be time to get out of this place." But any relief I felt was destroyed by his next words: "I've got some whisky in the cabin and the night is long."

What could I do? Say I needed something to eat? He would merely have waited for me in the cabin. Now I could see him clearly: a forceful, dominating man who radiated unshakable determination. Naturally I wanted to share the bill, but he dismissed the matter with a gesture and moved towards the door. I followed. We got into a crowded lift. The boat was teeming with people flocking round the fruit machines and sitting on the stairs. Their children were running all over the place and I was overcome by my old fear of crowds; when we finally reached the cabin I was trembling from head to foot. Mr Connaugh moved his luggage aside and took out a bottle of whisky, which he placed on the little table under the window. He had two silver cups as well. When he sat down the bunk creaked; it seemed altogether too puny and fragile for him. The cabin was first class, a bit of self-indulgence I'd allowed myself for this trip but which should have been reserved for me alone. It had a minibar, an elegant little arrangement which contained soft drinks, crisps and salted nuts. I opened its door.

"No," said Mr Connaugh, "not mineral water. Drink your whisky with plain water like the Scots. My father came from Scotland." I hurried to the bathroom and filled my toothmug, stumbling a little in the doorway, which had an unusually high threshold. "Ice?" I asked.

He shook his head. When he'd poured a little water into his whisky, he leaned back and drank. My voyage had suddenly been altered and my peace destroyed. I was sure he wouldn't go to bed for hours. "To you," he said. Everything repeats itself. "To you," I said.

"Journeys, journeys, forwards and backwards. And you know exactly where you're going, every time. Home and away again, away and home again."

"Not necessarily," I objected. "There are times..." but he interrupted me.

I'd thought of telling him that, so far as I was concerned, I hadn't booked any hotel and had no idea where I was going to end up. I wanted to give him a fairly adventurous picture of my new, virtually self-centred freedom, but he'd already launched into an account of his worries: wife, children, grandchildren, house and dog, the last-named having clearly died in very distressing circumstances. I closed up completely. Perhaps for the first time in my life, I effectively managed to shut off that dreadful compassion which has given both myself and those round me such fearful trouble. I use that word deliberately: fearful. Now perhaps you can understand why I started on my journey? Perhaps you have some idea of the depth of my fatigue, of my exhaustion and nausea in the face of this constant need to feel sorry for people?

Of course, one can't help feeling sorry for people. Every single one of us is afflicted by some secret, insurmountable disappointment, some form of anxiety or shame, and they sniff me out in no time. I mean, they know, their sense of smell leads them to me... Well, that's why I cleared off.

As I half-listened to Mr Connaugh I felt an enormous, and for me unaccustomed, anger gradually creeping over me. I emptied my glass and brutally interrupted him by saying, "Well, what d'you expect? Clearly you've driven them away by spoiling them. Or by scaring them! Why not let them be free to do what they want?" Maybe it was the effect of the whisky or whatever, but I added firmly: "Let go of them. The whole lot. And the house too!" But he was hardly listening and the photographs in his pocket book had appeared again.

Sometimes all manifestations of human anxiety seem very similar to me – at least, the everyday matters that people continue to worry about when, so to speak, rain is no longer coming in through the roof, there is no shortage of food and no one is being physically threatened – if you understand what I mean. Over and above factual catastrophes, miseries of one sort or another seem to repeat themselves with rather monotonous regularity so far as I've noticed: he or she is unfaithful or bored, someone's no longer enjoying their work, ambitions or dreams have gone out of shape, time's rapidly getting shorter, one's family is behaving in an incomprehensible and frightening way, a friendship has been totally poisoned by something trivial. One is frantically busy with inessentials, while what is important and irreparable goes from bad to worse, duty and blame nibble away at us and the whole syndrome is vaguely labelled angst, a spiritual malaise one seldom succeeds in defining or even tries to define. I know. One's opportunities for feeling ill at ease in life are countless and I recognise them; they constantly return, each affliction in its own little compartment. I should be familiar with this state of affairs and by now I should have found the right answer to the problem, but I haven't. There is no practical answer, is there? So we just listen. And anyway, it seems no one is really interested in practical solutions; they just go on talking, they come back and talk about the same thing again and again, they won't let you go. And here I was now sitting with Mr Connaugh, desperately trying not to feel sorry for him. It was going to be rather a long journey. At that particular moment he was holding forth about his misunderstood childhood.

The boat had begun to roll, but not too badly. I never get seasick, but I announced very clearly, "Mr Connaugh, I don't feel very well."

"Not Mr Connaugh," he said. "Albert. Didn't I say you should call me Albert? Well, that angst I was talking about..."

"Albert, I'm afraid I'm going to have to go up on deck. I need a little air; I'm not feeling well."

"No problem," he said. "What you need is a straight whisky now – instantly. And you can have all the air you want." He attacked our window – you know, the sort of cabin window they screw down firmly with goodness knows what kind of screw apparatus – but he got it open and a violent and extremely wet rush of ice-cold air took my breath away and blew the curtains horizontal while my glass fell to the floor. "Not bad," he said, much revived himself. "I've fixed it. Did you know I once dreamed of being a boxer? Now you'll feel better."

I reached for my overcoat.

"Albert," I said, "what is it you actually do?"

"Business," he answered shortly. My question had clearly depressed him again. There was a long silence. We raised our glasses to each other. Every now and then, salt spray drenched the table. I tried to say something funny about getting extra water in our drinks but it fell flat. To my horror I noticed Mr Connaugh's eyes were full of tears and his face was distorted. "You don't know," he said. "You don't know how it feels..."

It's when they start crying that I'm done for. I promise them anything – my friendship for life, money (though naturally not in this case), my bed – to undertake the most disagreeable tasks, and if it's a big strong man who's weeping... I get desperate. I leaped up and proposed God knows what – the nightclub, the swimming pool, anything – but the boat rolled, making me lose my balance so that I was flung violently against Mr Connaugh. He grabbed me like a drowning man and leaned his great head on my shoulder. It was terrible. From many points of view my position was extremely awkward. I've never known anything like it. Luckily the boat gave an enormous lurch at that moment and a lot of water came in through the window. Moving with lightning speed, Mr Connaugh rescued his bottle and set about screwing down the window as best he could. I rushed out into the corridor and escaped in blind flight through the bewildering open spaces of the boat.

When I eventually stopped, utterly exhausted, I was almost alone and it was completely silent. I looked in through an open door. Deck-places. Of course, a large room full of low chairs, most of them already tipped backwards for the night. A large number of deck passengers lying asleep rolled in blankets. I went in, very carefully picked up a spare blanket and chose a chair as far off as possible, against the wall. Wonderful. To be able to sleep and sink into silence, oblivious of everything... I'd developed a terrible headache and I was very wet, but that was nothing, nothing at all. I pulled the blanket over my head and vanished into a total disinterested peace.

When I woke I had no idea where I was. Someone was trying to pull the blanket off me and kept saying that it was her chair, it was number thirty-one and it was her chair and she had a ticket to prove it... I sat up, dazed and confused, and began saying, "Excuse me. I mean, it was a misunderstanding and the lighting's so bad, I really am very sorry..."

"Don't mention it," said the woman sourly. "I'm used to misunderstandings, that's exactly what they're always called."

My headache had got even worse and I was freezing cold. As far as I could see, nearly all the chairs were already occupied by sleeping people, so I just sat down on the floor and tried to massage my neck. "Haven't you got a ticket?" asked the woman severely.

"No."

"Have you lost it? This part of the boat's full, too."

I said nothing. Perhaps they'd let me sleep on the floor.

"Why are you wet?" she asked. "You smell of whisky. My son Herbert drinks whisky. Once he fell in the lake."

She sat and watched me with my blanket up under my chin. She was a bony little grey-haired woman, tanned and with small sharp eyes. She'd put her hat by her feet. She went on: "My suitcase is over there. Please bring it here if you can. It's best to have your things close beside you in a place like this. Mind the cake-box. That's for Herbert."

Afterwards, more people came in, looking for their chairs. The boat was rolling violently and not far off someone was being sick into a bag.

"It'll be different in London," said the old woman, pulling her suitcase nearer. "I just need to find out where Herbert is right now. D'you know where you have to go to find out people's addresses?"

"No," I said. "But perhaps the purser..."

"Are you going to sleep on the floor all night?"

"Yes. I'm very tired."

"I can understand." She added, "Whisky's expensive." And a little later: "Have you got any food in you?"

"No."

"I thought as much. There was food in the grill. But it was too expensive for me."

I huddled on the floor, buttoned up my overcoat and tried to sleep. It didn't work. How could this person go all the way to London without even knowing her son's address? And they'd be sure to stop her when she landed; these days you had to give references and prove you had enough money before they'd let you in... Where was she from? Somewhere in the country... She'd baked a cake for that son of hers... My God, how helpless and unpractical can you get!

I slept for a bit and woke again. She was snoring and had thrown an arm over the edge of the chair, her hand looked tired, a wrinkled brown hand with broad wedding and engagement rings. Now lots of people were being sick here and there round the room and the stench was frightful. I decided to go up on deck. My old dislike of lifts came over me at that moment, so I went up the stairs and passed the grill. People were still sitting and eating there. I hesitated a moment, then bought several large sandwiches and a bottle of beer and went back down the stairs and managed to find the place I'd just come from. She was awake.

"No, but that was really kind," she said and immediately attacked the sandwiches. "Won't you have half?" But I wasn't hungry any more, and sat thinking about how much money she might need to be allowed to land. Wasn't there some sort of Christian hostel that looked after confused travellers? I must find the purser; perhaps he would know...

"My name's Emma Fagerberg," she said.

The person lying on the next chair emerged from under a blanket and said, "Shut up! I'm trying to sleep."

The other pulled out her handbag from under her pillow. "You've been so kind," whispered Mrs Emma Fagerberg. "I'll show you some photos of my son. This is what Herbert looked like when he was four. The picture's a little blurred, but I have several others which are much better... "

The Garden of Eden

WEST OF ALICANTE, one day in February, Professor Viktoria Johansson arrived in the mountain village where she had arranged to stay at her goddaughter Elisabeth's house. The village was small and very old, with narrow close-built houses that climbed up the side of the mountain just as they did on the picturesque post-cards Elisabeth sent her from time to time.

It had been a long, tiring journey. Viktoria was a little disappointed that Elisabeth wasn't there to meet her at the airport as agreed. Perhaps not so much disappointed as astonished – they had been planning this trip for so long, and with such great anticipation. There was no doorbell. Viktoria knocked but there was no response, except that two multicoloured cats slunk down from a wall and meowed. So she took Elisabeth's spare keys from her handbag, unlocked the door and went through into a patio. Not a large one, but it looked exactly the way a patio should – a yard paved with stone, plants in neat rows of bulging clay pots, and over her head a roof of light greenery. Viktoria put down her bags and said to herself, "Aha. A patio." It was reassuring. It precisely matched her dream of this remote foreign country. As Elisabeth wasn't at home, Viktoria unlocked the next door. The room seemed very dark after the strong sunshine. Its single window was small and framed a view of bright green leaves and oranges. You could lean out and pick one, thought the weary Viktoria – if, in fact, it really was Elisabeth's tree and not the neighbour's. There was total silence. Now she saw that the room was in great disorder – clothes, papers, the remains of a meal, everywhere signs of anxiety and haste – and in the middle of the table, a letter.

She read it without sitting down: "Dear Godmother, Just heard that mother is seriously ill, catching a plane immediately. Hope you can manage, terribly sorry to leave you like this. If the gas canister runs out, José at the café in the square can help, also with firewood, he speaks a little French. In haste, love Elisabeth. PS Would have written but it wouldn't have reached you in time."

Poor child, thought Viktoria – with Hilda going and falling ill right at this moment. But she was rather frail even all those years ago. The hills were too much for her, that time we went to Scotland. That must have been 19... Anyway, we were very young. Such a whiny companion. We used to talk about going to "the land where the lemon-trees bloom", or to Spain. I'll write to her. And to Elisabeth. But there's no rush, one thing at a time. I wonder how you light the gas.

She took off her hat. Sitting on a straight-backed chair in Hilda's severe whitewashed room, she tried to remember more about her childhood friend. But Hilda grew hazier and hazier, hardly more than a little prick of conscience. She lit her third cigarette of the day and busied herself studying the window with the oranges.

Viktoria Johansson had been a very popular teacher in her day. She had known how to hold people's attention. Her sudden silences had nothing to do with absent-mindedness; they indicated the shaping of some idea that needed to be presented with absolute clarity. Later, too, at the university where she lectured on Nordic Philology, she commanded great respect, despite her mildness and total inability to find fault or control her papers and notes, which she was constantly losing or leaving behind. Perhaps what disarmed her students was her impractical helplessness and the invariable benevolence that misinterpreted every attempt at opposition or mockery. Even at a distance she inspired a sense of security, a small stable figure approaching calmly in snub-nosed shoes. She liked to go about in a trench coat and roomy, comfortable clothes, though she did have a chinchilla evening cape and real pearls. She would wear her pearl necklace whenever students came to visit her at home.

Even before she taught at the university she'd been in the habit of giving a little party for her pupils once a week. In those days she served hot chocolate and pastries; later they got Martini and olives and were allowed to bring a friend if they liked. There were those who thought it was all a bit over the top, but they gave in to Viktoria's utter lack of pretension. She wasn't there to be judged; just observed and accepted.

When young people came to Viktoria's parties, they would make bets about what it would be that she'd need their help with. It became a kind of game. Maybe she couldn't get the cork out of a bottle of vermouth, or maybe the flat was too dark because a fuse had blown and she didn't know how to fix it, or there would be a window she couldn't close, or an important paper had slipped down behind the bookcase. It was with a certain tenderness that they would sort things out, then laugh and say, "Dear old Viktoria!" Elisabeth had perhaps not been one of her best students, but she was very sweet and lovable.

Elisabeth had got Hilda's room upstairs ready for Viktoria – a dressing gown spread out on the bed, a spray of almond blossom, an ashtray. And, most thoughtful of all, an Erle Stanley Gardner. The dear child had not forgotten Viktoria's weakness for murder mysteries.

This window too was very small, but from here she could see the terraces climbing the mountainside higher and higher with long curving pink and white rows of flowering almond trees. Elisabeth had explained to her how the terraces held the soil in place and how they had been maintained for hundreds of years; though nowadays not many people knew how to build walls the old way, every stone fitted into place without mortar like the finest intarsia. Viktoria was particularly interested in walls. Once, out at the seashore at home, she had tried to repair a stone pier, but if you're not good with your hands then, sadly, you're just not.

There was one more little staircase. It led up to a rooftop terrace, from where the wide landscape's incredible beauty suddenly opened out. Mountain ranges rose all round in massive majesty, so that from here in the deep bowl of the valley, Viktoria felt no larger than a flea. A dramatic landscape, enormous and enclosed. What effect did it have on human beings? It was so utterly solitary. She stood still and listened, gradually becoming aware of how the silence was accentuated by never being absolute: now and then a dog barked, a car passed on the road below the village, church bells rang a long way off. Points of comparison, she thought, like the way the ocean grows larger if there are islands breaking the horizon. We need contrast, she told herself. And now, I think this taxing day has gone on long enough. I won't unpack or make myself anything to eat. I'll just go to bed.

Viktoria slept peacefully, her dreams great images full of mystery. Cocks started crowing before dawn; it sounded like there were a lot of them in the village. Then it was morning. The room was horribly cold, especially the stone floor. She put on all the woollen clothes she had and went downstairs. She opened the window with the oranges, leaned out and took an orange in her hand, but could not bring herself to pick it – somehow it felt wrong. Better to have a cup of tea.

Thank goodness the gas worked; the canister wasn't empty. There was another device, maybe something to do with hot water. Viktoria carefully turned a knob and it sprang into action with an alarming hiss, so she switched it off again and made her tea. The refrigerator was full of neat little plastic packages. She opened one but, suspecting it contained deep-frozen squid, she hastily closed it again. The jam jar looked just the way it should. Perhaps it was the ordinariness of the jam jar that disturbed her; she was intruding in someone else's life, in another woman's refrigerator, her bed, her distressed departure. I'm being selfish. What do I know about Elisabeth? There was a safety razor in the bathroom: perhaps a man had to move out because of me.

Viktoria put on her hat and coat, poured a saucer of milk for the cats and went out. The morning was chilly; the sun had barely risen above the crest of the mountain. The village street ended in the square, a pretty little place with a pump in the middle and several trees which had not yet put out leaves; she must find out what they were. Plane trees perhaps? There was the shop, and José's Café and a big yellow letterbox that seemed a safe and homely object to Viktoria. She needed to buy stamps somewhere and send scenic postcards to some of her old students. All the doors were still closed. An old man crossed the square and they greeted each other. I live here now, thought Viktoria with a little thrill of pleasure, and people say hello to me when they pass... Everything's going to be all right.

Back in the shade of the patio she buried herself in her *Guide for Tourists: Useful Phrases*: "Please. I'm sorry. Excuse me. Where can I find a shoeshine, tailor, souvenir shop, beauty salon?"

At twelve there was a knock on the door and a young man came in with a toolbox, smiled and explained something Viktoria didn't understand. Then he began making a large hole in the wall. It's funny, you think you've learned all these fine and useful things to say in Spanish, but when you need them they all just vanish. She gave the young man some of Elisabeth's wine and a cigarette and fussed around him until the hole was finished. Then he left. A little later he came back, and with another nice smile presented Viktoria with an entire mimosa bush. She was overcome. Mimosa was a thing you bought in tiny sprigs for people's birthdays. It was as if this foreign land had accepted her. It was unbelievable – she must remember to tell Elisabeth.

Now the young man filled the hole with plaster. Then he cleared up after himself, looked at her, and laughed.

"Very good work," said Viktoria shyly. "Very, very good."

When there was a knock on the door the next day, Viktoria thought the young man must have come back, perhaps to do more work on the wall, but it was a red-haired woman who spoke English and was looking for Elisabeth. She had four small dogs.

"How nice!" exclaimed Viktoria. "Please do come in! What a lot of little dogs. Do sit down. I'm so sorry, Elisabeth isn't here; the poor child has had to go home because her mother's been taken ill. I'm her godmother, Viktoria Johansson. May I offer you a cup of tea?"

"Josephine O'Sullivan," said the visitor. "Thanks, but maybe not tea, I don't want to put you to any trouble. But Elisabeth usually has some wine in her kitchen cupboard."

Viktoria went and looked in Elisabeth's cupboard and found half a bottle of whisky.

The dogs were lying close beside Josephine's chair, and after a while two of them jumped up on her lap.

"Cheers," said Viktoria, who didn't like whisky. "Have you lived here long, Miss O'Sullivan?"

"Only a year. But most of the colony have been here much longer."

"The colony?"

"Yes, the English colony. And a few Americans. It's so cheap here."

"And so beautiful," added Viktoria. "So peaceful; a real paradise!"

Josephine laughed, screwing up her small face which made her look older. She pushed the dogs off her lap and emptied her glass.

"They seem very attached to you," Viktoria said. "Would you like a little more?"

"Yes, thank you."

"A cigarette?"

"Thanks, I've got my own." Josephine said nothing for a long time. She lit her cigarette, drew on it several times, then stubbed it out irritably in the ashtray. "Paradise, you say. We've our snakes here too, you know! It's not safe to walk about in the village any more. And no one does anything about it."

"But the Spaniards…" Viktoria began.

Josephine interrupted impatiently. "You wouldn't understand," she said. "But please, don't you worry about it."

One of the dogs jumped up on her lap again, while the others squeezed in under her chair.

Viktoria said, "I'm so sorry Elisabeth's not here. Is there anything I can help you with?"

"No. You wouldn't understand."

Several motorcycles passed, then it was quiet again.

Suddenly Josephine broke out vehemently, "No one cares! No one!"

The smallest dog started barking.

"Sit!" Josephine shouted. "Sit! You and your paradise! If someone had sworn to kill you, how would you feel!?"

Now all the dogs began yapping.

Viktoria said, "Don't you think we ought to let them out?"

When she had taken the dogs to the patio and come back, her visitor was standing at the window with her back to the room. Viktoria waited.

"Her name is Smith," Josephine continued, speaking quietly with her lips pressed together. "Smith, if you please. She goes round the village brandishing a knife and threatening to murder me. And she lives right next door to me with only a single wall between us! She hates dogs and stereos, she sticks threatening letters under my door and makes faces at my cleaning woman, and last week she cut down my mimosa! I went to the police but they said they can't do anything until something has actually happened, in other words, until I'm lying there with my throat cut!"

"Was it a large mimosa?" Viktoria asked.

Josephine gave her an angry look. "A metre high," she snapped.

"And what do the dogs have to say about it?"

"They bark, of course."

"My dear Miss O'Sullivan, let's not be too hasty. Murder is a very big word; it should only be used with care and forethought. It's quite chilly in here. What about a fire? I think Elisabeth has some firewood out on the patio."

The wood turned out to be big chunks of olive and some sort of hairy brushwood. Josephine got the fire lit and it burned with an intense blue flame.

"It burns so beautifully," said Viktoria. "Differently. Not like at home."

Josephine stood still and gazed into the fire. "No," she said, "not like at home."

Viktoria remembered times when students had come to her to talk about something terrible that had happened to them. It used to help a bit to let them light a fire in her tiled stove.

"Miss O'Sullivan," she said, "I want to think seriously about your problem and try and find a way to help you. But you'll have to let me give it some careful thought."

Josephine turned to Viktoria. Her whole bearing changed and relaxed. The tension went out of her face and she whispered, "Will you really help me? Seriously? I can count on it, can't I?"

"Of course you can," said Viktoria. "This has to be dealt with. But right now you go home and think about something else." She was on the point of adding, "Read a nice murder mystery." But she caught herself at the last moment.

When Josephine and her dogs had gone, Viktoria took out paper and a pen, lit a cigarette and settled down in front of the fire. She felt quite revived. First she wrote "The Josephine Case", then after thinking a bit changed it to "The Woman with the Knife".

1. I shall call the woman with the knife X, which is better than Smith. Is it X or J who's demented? Or both? (NB: police no good, they won't help).

2. Find out if it's legal in Spain to run about threatening people with knives. She could at least be fined for disorderly conduct but that might make her even more belligerent. What sort of knife has she chosen? Stiletto? Kitchen knife? This would seem to be an important detail, at least psychologically. What do I know about X? Nothing.

3. Motive. Dogs and stereo aren't enough; there must be something else, something more significant. Discover the motive.

4. Method. Must make contact with X. Is this urgent? Or is J being melodramatic? Have a word with José, but be diplomatic.

The fire burned well, and the room was soon hot.

Viktoria decided since everyone here took a siesta in the middle of the day, she could do the same with a clean conscience. An excellent custom that should be introduced in Scandinavia.

She paid José a visit at the café. She gave him her card and presented his wife with a box of chocolates originally meant for Elisabeth. While José served her coffee, she talked a little about the weather and the beauty of the landscape and asked him if he had any contact with the foreigners in the village.

He shrugged his shoulders. "They keep to themselves," he said. "Pensioners. Mostly women, you understand, they live longer."

"What do they do with themselves?"

"They go to parties at each other's houses," said José with a grin.

Viktoria mentioned that she had the name of one of the women, a Miss Smith, and that maybe she would call on her one day.

"Really?" said José. "You actually mean it?" He turned to his wife, who was standing behind the counter listening: "Catalina, have you heard the news; the Professor here is going to call on Miss Smith!"

"God help her," said Catalina. "She'll never get into the house."

Viktoria had to climb a horribly long flight of steps to reach the building where Josephine lived right next door to X. When she got there, she sat down on a low wall with her Spanish phrasebook and waited. It was a very long time before she saw X come out of her house, lock the door, and stand still as if unsure which way to go. She had a shopping bag with her, so presumably was on her way to the shop. She was very small and didn't look particularly dangerous, just gloomy. Her hair was grey and she had made no effort whatsoever to do it up. No sign of a knife. Finally she came towards Viktoria.

"Excuse me," said Viktoria. "I'm not feeling at all well. Where could I get a little water?"

"There's a pump in the square," X answered, her eyes suspicious and very dark.

"But I'm not sure I can make it that far. It's the heat – I'm not used to it."

And so Viktoria got into the narrow little house where X lived. Now she really did feel ill, for she wasn't used to telling lies.

X placed a glass of water in front of her and went back to the door. After a while she asked if Viktoria was feeling better.

"I'm afraid not," said Viktoria truthfully. "I'm so sorry, you've been very kind, but couldn't you sit down with me for a moment? I hope I haven't got sunstroke…"

X sat down on a chair near the door.

"I'm not used to the heat," Viktoria went on. "Do you know if anyone else in the colony has had sunstroke?"

"No," said X scornfully. "But if they had, it wouldn't surprise me. Half the time they do nothing but sunbathe."

"And the other half?"

"Parties. You'll find out. They drink cocktails and gossip and jabber away about nothing at all. Another week and you'll be right at the centre of it, you're just the sort they like."

"Dear me," said Viktoria. "It sounds dreadful."

X put down her shopping bag and spoke with quiet intensity. "Yes, it is dreadful. They invade one deserted house after another and fix them up. All mod cons inside – but the outside has to look primitive and romantic. These people and their easy lives! They swarm like hornets with their cars and their lapdogs. Like a plague of locusts! I've been here from the start, twenty years. I've seen it all! They undermine everything."

"Like fig trees," said Viktoria.

"I beg your pardon?"

"Fig trees. My goddaughter Elisabeth told me that fig trees have roots that spread a very long way and can destroy walls and roads, whatever. They crowd out everything else."

"Exactly," said X. "They crowd out everything else. You just don't know where you belong any more." She got up and stood waiting by the door.

On her way home Viktoria tried to imagine what it must feel like to be a total outsider. This was not a new problem to her. Students excluded from the lives of their fellow students used to come and ask her what to do. Very disturbing, really complicated. She tore up her notes about The Woman with the Knife. But the case was by no means solved; it had just entered a new phase.

Next morning Josephine arrived with all her dogs, and before she was even through the door burst out, "Professor, dear Professor Viktoria. I heard you've been to see her. What did she say about me?"

"Nothing."

"But she must have said something!"

Viktoria patted the smallest, most neurotic dog and said, "I think she's just terribly lonely."

"Is that all?" said Josephine, raising her voice. "She's lonely – is that all you've found out? I could have told you that at the start. But why does she hate me in particular, that's what I want to know!"

"My dear Miss O'Sullivan," said Viktoria, "calm down. I'm only just beginning this investigation." And then she was angry with herself. Investigation, she thought, such a pretentious word. I've been reading too many murder mysteries... She went on quickly, "People get hold of the wrong end of the stick, you know, often for some very unimportant reason – say a disappointment – and then the problem just grows and grows till it's out of control..."

Josephine grew vehement. "Are you defending her? What are you trying to tell me? All right, she's lonely! That's not my fault! You promised..."

"Yes I know, I promised. Sit down. How about a little whisky?"

"Maybe a small one," said Josephine angrily. "But just a very small one. I'm on my way to the Wainwrights."

"They're having a party?"

"Yes, they're having a party."

"Listen to me," said Viktoria. "I've been looking for a motive and I think I've found one. She's made you into some sort of symbol."

But Josephine wasn't listening. She was talking about Lady Oldfield, who would very much like to invite the Professor to her reception next Thursday, an intellectual gathering, just the inner circle. They were not all averse to enlarging the colony.

Then invite X, thought Viktoria angrily. I want no part of their colony. They can enlarge it some other way.

Suddenly Josephine stopped talking and stared at Viktoria. "What's wrong?" she said. "Why are you looking at me like that? Don't you want to help me any more?"

"Of course I do. But try to understand. Miss Smith has serious problems."

"I see," Josephine interrupted. "You're defending her! You have to get it into your head – she's dangerous! Don't believe her. She's a witch; she twists everything, turns black into white. I know her! I forbid you to see her."

Viktoria felt herself turning red in the face. She opened her mouth to speak but was interrupted again. "Yes, yes, I know what you're going to say, but there's no point in talking to her. Go and see the police if you want to help, or go to the mental hospital in town! She's mad, she needs taking in hand!"

One of the dogs started barking.

"Miss O'Sullivan," said Viktoria very deliberately, "perhaps we should return to the subject another time. You must excuse me. I have an important letter to write."

That was unfriendly, she thought. I let myself take offence, which wasn't necessary. But who is this Josephine, hardly even middle-aged, to jump all over me like this, forbidding me to do what I think is right! Nonsense. I have every right to be angry. I need to remember – there's not as much difference as people think between the young and the old. One of them's excluded, one of them's trying to remain included, none of it's going well. Mad, she says. Mad – needs taking in hand. There is more than one way of taking someone in hand.

Dear Hilda,
Here in your beautiful home, so many memories come back to me from our travels in Scotland and Ireland so

long ago. Do you remember the time we picked spring flowers somewhere near Galway and put them in a jam jar on the window ledge? The other day I found the first spring flowers by the roadside but they didn't like...

No. No good. Too sentimental. How ill is she really?

Dear Hilda,
It's so peaceful and pleasant here...

But now Hilda was going hazy again.

We could have talked to each other more. Those trips weren't any fun at all, but we could have discussed it and tried to figure out why things went wrong – was she inhibiting my freedom, my happy curiosity, or was it me who frightened her into helpless whining? Very interesting, actually.

Maybe I'll write to her a little later.

Viktoria went and knocked on X's door with no idea what she wanted to say. X let her in, silently, her face totally closed.

"Good afternoon," said Viktoria. "I had no real reason for coming. I just wanted to come."

"Ah, paying a call," said X. "A social call, if I understand you correctly. Have you joined their colony?"

"No. I think it suits me better to stay on the outside."

"Sit down. Can I get you something to drink?"

"No, thank you, not today. Nothing."

After a long silence, X said, "And no conversation? Not a word? No crumb of comfort for the recluse?"

"That word doesn't suit you," Viktoria said. "But you have every right to your solitude. Anyway, solitary people interest me. There are so many different ways of being solitary."

"I know just what you mean," said X. "I know exactly what you're going to say. Different kinds of solitude. Enforced solitude and voluntary solitude."

"Quite," said Viktoria. "There's no need to go into it further. But when people understand one another without speaking, it can often leave them with very little to talk about, don't you think? I've had that experience, not often but once or twice. It felt good, a pleasant sort of silence."

Her hostess lit a table lamp. What am I doing, thought Viktoria. Am I being disloyal to Josephine? But all I want is to take this thing further, to explore, to understand in order to help.

"Tell me something," said X. "Are you a curious person?"

"Yes, you might say that. Or, rather, I'm interested."

"In me?"

"Certainly. In everything."

"Do you get the impression that I'm dangerous?"

"No, not really." Viktoria paused for a moment, then said, perhaps rashly, "Someone once gave me a pressure cooker. For making porridge, that sort of thing. It was dangerous and exploded. The inside pressure was apparently too great."

"Very likely," said X. "All that proves is that you shouldn't mess with appliances unless you know how they're made. What did you do with it?"

"What could I do? It was broken. Such a pity, such a fine appliance."

"There she goes again," said X. "Opera. That's all she has. I detest opera."

The music from next door was amazingly clear.

"Do you like opera?"

"Not particularly," said Viktoria. "What I like best is New Orleans, and classic jazz. When I retired, my students gave me a stereo. I take good care of it." Viktoria took out her cigarettes and looked enquiringly at X.

"Feel free," said her hostess, a little impatiently. Then there was silence.

At last X spoke again. "Do you even know why you came to see me?"

Viktoria didn't answer.

"You seem to be an honest sort of person. You're naturally open. But you've come to the wrong place; you need to be careful. This is a dangerous place for people like you."

"What you mean is", said Viktoria carefully, "that perhaps I'm too suggestible?"

"More or less."

"And that I might find it hard to take a stand and be decisive?"

"You're very wise," said X.

Viktoria sighed, stubbed out her cigarette and got to her feet.

"I'll think about it," she said. "It's a terrible climb up the hill to your house. But it's always easy to get down again."

By now it was dusk. Viktoria walked over to the low wall at the edge of the village's final ridge. There they were again, those lovely columns of blue smoke rising in the shadow of the mountain straight up into the windless evening air. They must be burning leaves and dry branches, the way they did at home in spring.

Yes, I have to be careful, I have to know what I want and who I'm trying to protect. She was quite right. I'll go home now and teach myself some Spanish. How do you say: "Excuse me, is there anyone who can help me with my laundry?"

One evening Viktoria set off in a new direction, following her nose. The lane turned into a path that gradually disappeared into a stony landscape full of olive trees that seemed tremendously old. Dead branches still hung on the trees. Under the olives a flock of sheep were grazing – parallel dirty-yellow backs, bowed heads, the submissive posture of victims. She caught her foot in a plastic bag and saw she was in a kind of rubbish dump, the unavoidable outskirts of any human paradise. She felt irrationally depressed.

At that exact moment the setting sun broke through a gap in the mountain chain and the twilit landscape was instantly transformed and revealed; the trees and the grazing sheep enveloped in a crimson haze, a sudden, beautiful vision of biblical mystery and power. Viktoria thought she had never seen anything so lovely. She remembered once a set designer saying, "My job is to paint with light, that's all it is. The right light at the right time." The sun moved quickly on, but before the colours could fade, Viktoria turned and walked slowly back to her house.

Dear Hilda,

I just want to say hello because I feel so happy this evening. Your Spanish landscape is so much more than I ever expected or dreamed of, and I dream more often and more powerfully than anyone knows. Couldn't we spend a little time here together when you're well again?

I'm not sure we handled our trips together the way we might have, and I think it was mostly my fault. Trying to do and see everything, rushing here and there the way I did. I know better now.

You know it's possible just to be in a place, to look around until you actually see, differently, and then to talk about it, talk about anything at all and feel our way forward together. The young are always in too much of a hurry, don't you think?

Promise me we'll try again. Please?

A big hug from Viktoria.

On Sunday morning Viktoria woke up to bells – the distant admonishment of church bells. Maybe that's a good idea, she thought. For once. But just as she was putting on her shoes, she caught sight of her hiking boots standing in a corner, and she thought some more. Such a beautiful morning. And it had really been unenterprising of her not to have discovered where the main road led, the big main road below the village. Church could wait for a cloudy day. So she pulled on her boots and packed a bag with a bottle of fruit juice, cigarettes, and her *Guide for Tourists: Useful Phrases*. If the expedition proved tiring it might be nice to lie on the grass in the shade of an orange tree and read.

The morning was still cool and beautiful. On either side of the road were big orchards, their branches bowed to the ground with oranges and lemons, perfect Gardens of Eden – except that they were surrounded by fences. Inside, no one moved among the trees, where the grass grew tall and utterly untouched. When she came to a gate, it was locked. Viktoria thought that with a little effort she could probably slip quickly through the fence and creep under the branches as if into a green grotto and lie there hidden from the world, picking an orange now and then – and, of course, putting the peel in her pocket...

A woman was walking toward her from the village, a woman in black. It was X.

"Good morning!" called Viktoria. "Are you on your way into town? May I walk with you?"

X stopped for a moment. "No," she answered. "Not today."

"I've been doing a lot of thinking," Viktoria began, but X turned away and walked on down the valley. It was as if a black raven had sailed by in the sunshine. Viktoria was hurt; after all, they had had a very personal conversation in which X had definitely come out on top. She could have been a little more pleasant.

Women, thought Viktoria, difficult at school from the very first class. Boys were easier; you knew where you stood with them. She sat down by the roadside, took out her bottle of juice and her *Guide for Tourists* and started thinking about the road home, all uphill. It was getting too hot again now. It was always either icy cold or too hot.

A car came driving down from the village and stopped and hooted; a door slammed open and out came Josephine with her dogs. She staggered and sat down laughing in the road. "Mrs Viktoria!" shouted someone from inside the car. "Come with us to the fiesta! Carnival! Hurry up, they may have started already!" Josephine's face looked even smaller framed between two plaits of her astonishingly red hair. She had a ribbon over her head and glass beads round her neck and, as far as Viktoria could judge, was meant to look like a Red Indian. There was a knife in her belt. She shouted, "You're my prisoner, Professor!"

Viktoria stood up and asked if it was a real carnival.

"The biggest one all year," Josephine assured her. "Everyone does just what they want, and to hell with everybody else, just footloose and fancy-free! Hurry up; we haven't got all day! We stopped at your place but you weren't there. This is Mabel and Ellen and Jackie. Here, have a tipple of this! We're going to a party!"

It was whisky again. They drove down the hill at a dizzying speed. One of Josephine's friends had started singing. Viktoria looked out anxiously for X; it wouldn't do at all for X to see her with Josephine, in the bosom of the colony, deserting to the enemy camp. She crouched down and tried to make herself invisible, thinking bitterly, What do I mean, deserting? Which way? If Josephine had seen me walking down the road with X, what would she have thought? And anyway, does it really matter what they think?

Down in the town they were met by music.

"Another small drop, Viktoria," said one of the colonists.

"No, thanks. Maybe not right now."

They left the car and made their way slowly through the crowds in the narrow streets. Josephine clung to Viktoria's arm, shouting cheerfully, "Make way! Make way! I've captured a real professor!"

It was extremely embarrassing.

Balloons everywhere, shouts and laughter. Small children riding through the crowds on their fathers' shoulders, a howling cherub in a bright yellow wig, a miniature devil with horns, a Zorro, clouds of confetti rising from the square ahead.

"Please, Miss O'Sullivan," Viktoria pleaded, "let go. I really don't need to go any closer." But she was pushed on relentlessly, tightly hemmed in by a strange procession of colour and movement under a rain of flowers and sprigs of olive. Many of the dancers were wearing masks, violent faces of mockery, ecstasy, unbearable pain. To Viktoria their gestures seemed out of control, their colours chosen to hurt the eye – and now they were approached by tight, silent rows of children in costume. Viktoria's eyes fastened on a solemn little girl and with a thrill of recognition she told herself, Yes, that's the Infanta of Velázquez. So beautiful. The Inquisition marched by, followed by the Most Beautiful Of All under an arch of mimosa and almond blossom. Viktoria thought she looked frightened. Then came the cobwebbed figures of the Dead Forest, followed by several marching whisky bottles. Viktoria turned to smile at Josephine, but Josephine had vanished.

I must try and describe all this to Hilda. I'll write this very evening; it'll cheer her up. Just look, all these people getting to live out their dreams, play a part, finally become someone else. It's wonderful. Why don't we have carnivals at home – my goodness, we certainly need them. Here's a woman whose dream was to be a brave and gallant Robin Hood: look at the long feather in her hat! And those excited men dancing their dream of being women, with their glorious bosoms!

The music grew wilder. She saw a toreador and his bull playing a passionate game with each other. People shouted and pressed forward. It was a splendid fiesta!

A black sedan full of bandits rolled into the square. And in front of it, on an empty patch of naked street, there was X – dancing, as dark as the car, slashing the air round her with a long, gleaming knife. A kitchen knife, in fact. The music had changed to España Cañi. Then Viktoria saw Josephine rush out into the street – Josephine, also with a knife in her hand. "Josephine!" she cried. "Stop! Come back!"

The two women circled each other in front of the bandits' car. They lunged, retreated, and the crowd cried bravo and clapped hands in time with the music. Viktoria shouted again, "Stop! *Pericoloso*! Dangerous!"

But no one paid her any attention. The two women had begun to stamp on the ground, approaching each other, circling close and dancing away again. Their dance had now captured the crowd's complete attention. Josephine was having difficulty staying on her feet. Someone behind Viktoria said they weren't doing the right steps and weren't really Spanish at all. Viktoria turned round and hissed, "Shut up, you idiot! You don't understand what's going on! This is a matter of life and death."

The procession moved slowly on and Viktoria followed, pushing forward, unapologetically. She saw Josephine stagger and drop her knife. X picked it up and gave it back to her, and they continued circling each other like cats in a back yard. Josephine's dogs ran back and forth as close to X as they dared and yapping as if possessed. And the music played on. But now the procession had slowed and stopped. Josephine staggered against the radiator of the bandits' car and clung to it with both hands. X advanced on her slowly and Viktoria shrieked, "No!" X raised her knife and quickly, with a couple of slashes, she sliced off Josephine's red braids, threw them contemptuously on the street and walked away.

The crowd drew back to let her pass; it had all happened very quickly. The music switched to "Never on Sunday" and Viktoria was suddenly trapped in the tightly packed crowd and wanted only to go home. Eventually she managed to escape from the square to some deserted streets and sat down outside a café to rest her legs. A man came up and said, "Sorry to bother you. I'm American. You called me an idiot."

"And so you were," said Viktoria wearily. "When someone is stamping her feet, it doesn't make any difference whether or it's 'Spanish' or not. People stamp their feet because they're angry. Where do you think I could find a taxi?"

"My car's just around the corner," the man said. "I'm from Houston, Texas."

All the way up to the village he told her about his family and his job. They exchanged addresses and promised to send postcards.

Stretched on her bed in the cool darkness Viktoria tried to make sense of what had happened. The vendetta had clearly reached a dramatic climax. And now, thought Viktoria, Josephine will just have to find a new way to do her hair – and X will be even more unpopular and isolated. She's the loser, she behaved badly. I must try to be fair. It's natural to root for the underdog, but what does sympathy have to do with justice? Josephine was the one I promised to help. But X interests me more – I'm not objective.

It was the same way with my students – it mattered so much to them which side I was on. They would drive me to despair by seeing everything in black and white. Is there such a thing as a real absolute, a true either/or? Or is everyone somehow right in their own way, and because I understand that, it makes me indecisive and wishy-washy, trying to tolerate each point of view? But those parties I used to give for my students were an attempt, perhaps an awkward one, or too timid, but an attempt nonetheless, to get them out of their tight little cliques and be friendly and civilised and listen and understand each other a little better. My parties were a good idea. I think I should try it again. A party for the whole colony? No. Just for Josephine and X.

The telegram came later that evening. 'Mum died this morning just fell asleep but it seems strange don't worry tell Jose if roof leaks dont worry Elisabeth.'

At first Viktoria felt she ought to go home and help. But maybe not. She sat at the table and read the telegram over and over. What was that about the roof? Why should it start to leak? How peculiar. After a while, she went up onto the terrace and emptied a couple of pailfuls of water on the roof. None of the water came through.

And then suddenly, with surprising intensity, Viktoria found herself grieving for the lost friend of her youth – Hilda, who never understood how easily she could have stopped being difficult.

I'll throw out that horrible squid! And take in the saucer I put out for the cats. They don't drink milk, these Spanish cats – not even the cats here are normal.

That evening Viktoria went to the café and ordered a Cuba Libre. She asked José what the wild cats drank when they were thirsty.

José laughed. "They lick up the dew."

That night Viktoria lulled herself to sleep by imagining she was an independent Spanish cat finding an opportune dew-cup at dawn (if dew-cups even grew in this country).

Viktoria wrote out invitations to her party, taking a lot of trouble with the formal wording and calligraphy.

The supper would take place at José's, the only restaurant in the village. It was behind his café, a terrace with a magnificent view over the valley, perfect for summer tourists passing through.

This will do nicely, Viktoria thought, and went to discuss her plans with José. There were a lot of people in the café. She greeted José and Catalina and invited them to take a glass with her because she needed advice on an important personal matter. Catalina smiled and said no, thank you, she was too busy, but José carried two Cuba Libres to a table by the glass doors to the terrace. Viktoria came straight to the point. "I'm planning a formal supper with two guests and I want it to be a really good one. I have confidence in your culinary experience and I'd like to discuss the menu. Isn't lamb the right choice for the main dish?

"Definitely," said José, enthusiastically. "I suggest *cordero con guisantes.*"

"That sounds excellent," said Viktoria, nodding thoughtfully as if she were an expert. And as a starter – I mean *entremeses?*"

"How about *gambas fritas?*"

Viktoria knew *gambas* were prawns. She made a dismissive gesture; people always had prawns at formal dinners back home. "Perhaps something more – exotic?"

"*Erizos naturales?*"

"Well, it depends," said Viktoria cryptically, not wanting to ask for a translation. "But we must have mimosa on the table, masses of it. Not almond blossoms, we have to think about the poor almonds. And the wine?"

"*Privilegio del Rey*," José answered firmly. "*Privilegio del Rey* without a doubt. Would you like to taste it, Professor? It's very renowned."

"With pleasure."

José fetched two large glasses and Viktoria tasted the wine. She nodded graciously and asked about the vintage. They continued their earnest discussion. The villagers followed the conversation carefully; they could tell it was very important.

José asked, "Which would you prefer, Professor, *ensalada verde mezclada* or *chalotas y remolachas?*"

"*Ensalada verde* of course."

"Of course," agreed José appreciatively.

"And cheese," said Viktoria.

"Just cheese? No dessert?"

"I think just cheese is more elegant. And then coffee."

José lifted his hands. "My dear Professor, that's impossible, unthinkable! You can't have a real supper without *postre! Crema de Café Dolores yanes, pastel infanta, platanos a la Canaria, amor frío...*"

"Is it so very important?" asked Viktoria in astonishment. "What was that last one called?"

"*Amor frío.*"

"Doesn't that mean more or less 'cold love'?"

"More or less."

"Then it couldn't be better," said Viktoria, and giggled. "Only one other important detail: there have to be oranges on the table, a large bowl. Complete with leaves." She could see that José didn't like the idea; he looked suddenly crestfallen. Then she took out her invitation cards and asked if he'd be so kind as to arrange for them to be delivered; it would be more polite than sending them by post.

Their conference was over.

The next day word went round that the unsociable professor was giving a dinner in style at José's. The detail about the oranges was considered highly amusing. And the combination of guests was a topic of general discussion. So far as anyone knew, neither woman had declined the invitation. Everyone could see that this completely altered the picture, which must now be judged from an entirely new angle, depending, of course, on the outcome of Viktoria's dinner.

The crucial evening itself was mild and beautiful. Viktoria dressed with particular care; the pearls were for her guests but the chinchilla was to impress the colony. The café was full of villagers but there was no one on the terrace. The colony was anxious not to appear inquisitive.

The guests arrived on time from different directions, Josephine without her dogs. Viktoria rose to welcome them. José appeared in a white apron and served *Privilegio del Rey*.

"So good of you to come," Viktoria said. "I'd like to drink to your health because, among other things, I believe you to be two very enterprising and courageous women. We'll raise our glasses to the spring, to new beginnings."

Josephine had been to a hair salon in town and was now crowned with an astoundingly large bush of red hair.

"How kind," she said. "How very kind."

Viktoria's guests were extremely wary; they looked as if they had come to take an examination.

Viktoria made a sweeping gesture encompassing the magnificent landscape, the mountains and the flowering valley and said, "You know, in the days when I had students, so many of them longed to travel, maybe to places like this, some time in the future when they'd be able to afford it. We often spread out a map of the world and talked about where we would most like to go. It was such fun." Viktoria turned to X and asked her how she had come to choose this particular village.

X shrugged and said, "For a long time I cared for an elderly relative. When she died I inherited her house."

"Do you ever feel homesick?"

"No. But I do sometimes think about lawns."

"Of course, lawns!" Viktoria energetically agreed. "And meadows. Here you can't get onto the grass; it's reserved for the orange trees. Of course, you could go into the mountains – there are no fences up there."

"It's nothing but stones," said Josephine. "I tried." She broke off as José came out on the terrace to serve them. When he'd gone, she repeated herself impatiently. "Nothing but stones. And it's so dark indoors. Always dark."

"Yes," said Viktoria. "But all you have to do is go outside. Am I right?"

Her guests didn't answer. There was a long silence. X was eating but Josephine merely toyed with her food.

Viktoria tried again. She told some amusing stories about her students, about her own impracticality, how they'd always lent a hand, the same way Josephine had helped her build a fire or the way Miss Smith had let her rest that time she was tired and feeling ill.

"You weren't feeling ill," X interrupted calmly and confidently. "You were perfectly fine. You were out sniffing around on her behalf."

"Quite true, Miss Smith," Viktoria answered lightly. "I behaved badly. But in all honesty, do you think it's proper to go around threatening to kill people and making faces at their cleaning lady?"

Josephine laughed and finally began to eat her food.

"As for you, Josephine O'Sullivan," continued Viktoria, determined to be fair, "is opera really the only music you've got?"

"No," said Josephine angrily.

José was there again, fussing about and asking if everything was satisfactory. "Thank you, absolutely perfect," Viktoria said. "Could we have another bottle of your excellent wine?" He bowed and went away. The wine came.

Viktoria looked out across the valley and said, "How quiet it is."

"Quiet," X remarked. "You've a weakness for quiet, haven't you? And there's no real need to talk if people are comfortable with not expressing every little thought. Wasn't that how you put it?"

Viktoria went red. "Any statement can lose its meaning if it's repeated in a distorted form," she said stiffly.

Josephine gave Viktoria a meaningful look, smiled sourly and shrugged.

The meal continued.

The oranges were beautifully arranged, each fruit still with its own green leaves. Viktoria picked one up and remarked that José had really done his best with them.

"An affectation," said X. "Does he think we're tourists? Nobody here eats oranges."

Viktoria said, "It was my idea, not José's. Think of the oranges as a decoration, a sort of symbol."

"Of what?"

"A dream perhaps, a symbol of the Tree of Knowledge in the Garden of Eden. Something unattainable. I absolutely believe in oranges."

"I so understand," Josephine exclaimed. "There's nothing wrong with having oranges on the table! In Russia they had apples. I know what Viktoria means. She's unusual."

"To put it mildly," said X very drily.

On the main road below the terrace, several small boys stopped and started pointing, shouting something in Spanish again and again.

"What do they want?" Viktoria said.

X looked at Josephine and explained carefully. "They're saying there's that woman who made a scene at the carnival, the one by the bandits' car."

"They don't mean me, they mean her!" Josephine shouted. "She was the one who went wild! Viktoria, you saw what happened!"

Viktoria had a sudden impulse to scold them. Girls, girls! she wanted to say, but she held her tongue. José came out and chased away the youngsters with a flood of animated Spanish.

The sun had dropped behind the mountains, and the evening chill set in as soon as it was gone. Viktoria was suddenly angry. "Ladies," she said, "for me the carnival was unbelievable. And I understand how the excitement could make anyone lose their head and go a bit wild. Believe me, I've lost control of myself more times than I like to remember. But afterwards I try to forget and hope others can do the same." She signalled to José to bring another bottle. "This is a very good wine. It should be drunk in a calm and thoughtful atmosphere. Ladies, what shall we drink to?"

"To you," Josephine burst out. "To justice! The justice that always wins out over foul play!" She had already had a few drinks before leaving home, just to be on the safe side.

"And how do you like her new hairdo?" said X, not touching her wine.

Viktoria corrected her. "How do I like Josephine's new hairdo? I think it makes her look younger."

She was rather tired now and decided to turn the party over to her guests. She excused herself and took refuge in the ladies' room. The view from that window was no less beautiful, but she hardly noticed. It was a bit cruel to leave the two of them together, she thought. I could have stayed. Now they're sitting there in silence. I've failed. I should have learned by now to let people sort out their own problems. I'm like some kind of sheepdog, running myself ragged to round everyone up and get them organised. The thought amused her. She decided to order some cognac with the coffee.

As she was going back through the café, José came up to her conspiratorially and whispered, "How's it going?"

"It's going fine, I think," Viktoria said. "It's working out. The food, the wine, the decoration – everything was perfect. I think we'll have some cognac with our coffee."

Her guests were sitting bolt upright. They had clearly been having a discussion.

"Dear Viktoria," said Josephine, breathless with excitement. "We've been thinking..."

"Thank her first," X broke in.

"Yes, of course. We'd like to thank you for your extraordinary kindness and generosity. A wonderful meal, so well thought out in every detail."

"Not so fast," said X. "Get a grip on yourself. Quite simply, Viktoria, you've given us a chance. But don't you think Josephine and I could just go on disliking each other?"

"It's possible," answered Viktoria. "Indeed, why not? But here's the cognac. What shall we drink to this time?"

"Nothing," said Josephine. "I've been talking too much. I really ought to go home. The dogs have been alone all evening."

"Their legs are too short," said X.

Viktoria raised her cognac and said, "Ladies, you waste your time on inessentials. When we've finished our coffee, I think we should devote ourselves to the contemplation of nightfall."

They walked through the café, where all conversation stopped, and came out onto the square.

"It's cold," said Josephine, trying to fasten Viktoria's chinchilla for her.

"Leave it alone," said X. "Viktoria knows whether she's cold or not. Stop fussing."

"You always know better than anyone else!" Josephine snapped. "But you don't know a thing about Viktoria, not a thing!" And she walked on ahead up the lane.

"Take no notice," said Viktoria. "She'll see things more clearly in the morning."

"You think so?"

"Of course. Everything can change." Viktoria did not explain in more detail that for her every new morning was a kind of happy challenge, just as it was with new opportunities, surprises, maybe even insights, yes, and plain excitement. In fact she'd done more than enough pontificating for one evening, and now she simply mentioned that José had promised to bring some firewood after nine. So she would sweep the patio and ask him to pile the wood in a different corner so it wouldn't disturb the bougainvillea.

X smiled. "Inessentials, my dear Viktoria. You mentioned inessentials, I think? All those tiny tasks and worries. Every new day filled with one thing or another. Look at Josephine up there. She spends half her day walking her dogs and playing her operas and the other half running to meaningless parties, and it's hard work being insulted, making yourself popular, clinging hard to what little pride you've got... And you, a real Viktoria, you condescend to display a well-meaning tolerance. Oh yes, I saw you in that car! Wait, don't say anything.

I know for someone like you it's hard to say no, but you have no real principles, not guiding ones that run consistently through everything you do. None of you have. You water down your drinks and your feelings. Do you understand what I'm saying? No single, firm, undiluted beliefs.

Walking on, they caught up with Josephine, who was sitting on the long flight of steps leading up to her house.

Viktoria said to X, "There are beliefs and beliefs. Hating the colony is not a particularly interesting one, and besides it's pretty diluted too by now, don't you think? You should find yourself a new one, a more useful one if you can. Or just forget it, of course."

"What do you mean, forget it?"

"Well, you could accept the fact that you're ordinary. I always find that quite exciting enough."

"Ha,ha, there you are," said Josephine. "Totally ordinary – like Viktoria. That's rare."

X helped Josephine to her feet and said, "Yes, yes, come on, let's go. Good night, Viktoria."

"Good night." For a moment Viktoria stood watching them climb the long, laborious flight of steps.

Many other people had been watching, too.

The next week X was invited to the Wainwrights'. And later even to Lady Oldfield's, though she wasn't accepted into the Inner Circle until the colony had assured itself that Miss Smith had interesting eccentricities that could contribute pleasantly to enlivening its social life. But that didn't happen till the autumn.

Shopping

IT WAS FIVE IN THE MORNING and still overcast. The dreadful stink seemed to be getting worse. As usual, Emily walked down Robert Street as far as Blom's grocery store. The shards of glass squeaked under her shoes and she decided that one day she'd have to make the place a little more approachable. So long as it didn't interfere with her constant shopping. They had plenty of canned food in the kitchen at the moment, but you could never be sure these days, Emily thought. Surprisingly, the big mirror was still there outside Blom's, and Emily stopped for a moment to tidy her hair. Really no one could call her fat now; plump might be more accurate – or Junoesque, as Kris liked to say. In fact her coat fitted a good deal better now; it was green and matched her shopping bags. She climbed a pile of rubble to get in through the window. Here it was rotting food that was smelling bad.

She noticed at once that they had been there again, because now the shelves were almost empty. They hadn't bothered with the sauerkraut; she stowed away what was left of that and helped herself to the last packet of candles and, while she was about it, a new washing-up brush and some shampoo. There was no more fruit juice, so Kris would just have to make do with river water, like it or lump it. She could go on to Lundgren's and have a look there, but that was quite a long way off. Another time. Wanting to make the most of her morning, Emily went into number six, left her bags near the entrance and walked up one floor to the Erikssons' flat. That was as far as you could go.

Luckily the Erikssons had not closed their door when they left. Emily knew there was nothing important left to take; she had shopped for all she wanted from there a long time ago, but it was nice to sit on the fine living-room sofa and rest her legs. Although of course it was no longer so fine any more, since others had stained it and cut it with knives. But Emily had got there first. And she'd had such great respect for the beauty of the peaceful room that she had taken nothing from it but food. Later, when everything had been trashed and soiled, she saved a few more things to brighten up the kitchen at home and to surprise Kris. This time she helped herself to the rococo wall-clock which had stopped at five, her shopping hour. No one else was out at five in the morning; it was a good safe time.

She started for home. She wondered whether Kris could eat sauerkraut, especially now his stomach was delicate. About halfway home she put down her bags, which were very heavy, and looked out over the changed landscape, the shrunken suburb where she lived. There certainly wasn't much left; on the other side of the river, nothing at all. Strange the trees hadn't yet burst into leaf in the park.

And then she caught sight of them, right at the far end of Robert Street, only two specks but moving, quite clearly moving. They were coming. She began to run.

The kitchen she shared with Kris was on the ground floor. They had always eaten at the kitchen table and had been about to have dinner when it happened. The rest of the floor was totally blocked. Kris had pointlessly injured his leg. In Emily's opinion he should never have rushed out, ending up with half the facade on top of him. It was nothing but idle male curiosity. He knew perfectly well what you were supposed to do. There had been warnings on the radio: "Stay indoors in the event of ..." and so on. And now here he was lying on a mattress Emily had found in the street.

She had hung the rug up to cover the hole where the window had blown out, and later fixed the whole thing in place by nailing up boards from rubbish she found outside. Luckily the toolbox had been in the kitchen. Otherwise, absolutely anyone could have climbed in through the window. To be really safe she spent hours piling up camouflage on the outside as well. As Kristian lay on his mattress listening to Emily constructing their defences, he couldn't help feeling that she was enjoying herself – at least up to a point. He took care not to alarm her. He spent a lot of time sleeping. This business of his leg didn't seem too serious but it did hurt and he couldn't rest his weight on it. The darkness distressed him more.

Now he was awake and groping for the candle and matches on the floor by the mattress. He lit the candle carefully so the match wouldn't go out. He had the books from the Erikssons' place, unread books from a world that had no meaning for him any more. He wound up his watch, as he did every morning. It was a little after six; she'd be home any minute. There weren't many matches left.

I wish we could talk about what's happened, thought Kristian; give it a name, have a serious matter-of-fact conversation. But I haven't the heart to. And I don't want to frighten her. If only we could have that damn window open.

Here she was. She unlocked the kitchen door, put her bags on the table, smiled at him and showed him the Erikssons' gilded clock, a monstrous object. "How's the leg? Had a good sleep?"

"Excellent," said Kristian. "Did you find any matches?"

"No. And there wasn't any more fruit juice. They've slashed the sofa at the Erikssons'."

"You're out of breath," said Kristian. "You've been running. Did you see them?"

Emily took off her coat and hung the new washing-up brush on the peg where the old one had been. "I must get some more water from the river so I can wash up," she said.

"Emily? Did you see them?"

"Yes. Only two of them. A long way off. Somewhere near Edlund's corner. Maybe people are moving to the centre now the shops are empty."

"Edlund's corner? But I thought you said it wasn't there any more? That there's nothing left beyond the petrol station?"

"Yes, yes, but the corner itself is still there." Emily put a plate with tomato juice and crispbread down beside him on the floor. "Try and eat something. You're getting much too thin." She took down the household book and entered the new cans of sauerkraut on the Vegetables page.

Very soon Kristian started talking about the window. They had to open it, free it up and let in the daylight again. He couldn't stand this darkness any longer.

"But they'll get in!" Emily exclaimed. "they'll find us in no time and take all the food I've been shopping for! Kris, please do try to understand. You have no idea what I've seen! The Erikssons' sofa... tons of smashed china, antiques as well... And anyway, it's so dark outside."

"How do you mean?"

"Well, it just keeps getting darker. Two weeks ago I could go shopping at four and now it's hard to see anything before five."

Kristian was very disturbed. "Are you sure? That it's getting darker? But it's the beginning of June – it can't be getting darker!"

"Kris, love. Calm down. It's just that it's always overcast. We haven't seen the sun since... I mean, not even once."

He sat up and took hold of her arm. "D'you mean like twilight or...?"

"No – I just mean it's overcast! Clouds, you know? Clouds! Why are you trying to upset me?"

Far off in the city the siren started up again. It sounded intermittently, with long intervals, a sort of helpless lament that made Emily frantic. Kristian had tried to reassure her by saying maybe they had a generator at the fire station that had somehow got stuck, but it was no use. She'd just wept, like she was doing now. Then she sprang up and began blindly rearranging her cans and jars on the kitchen shelf. One fell to the floor, rolled across and knocked over the candle, putting it out.

"Look what you've done," he said. "How many matches do you think we have left! What do you think we'll do when they're all gone – sit here in the dark and wait for the end? We've got to have that window open!"

"You and your window!" shouted Emily. "Why can't you just let me be happy? You know you like it when I'm happy! And we've got it nice here at home, haven't we? I found a bar of soap yesterday, you hear – a bar of soap!" Suddenly calm, she went on, "I'm making our home cosy and snug. I go out and shop. I find amazing things... Why do you have to scare me? Why do you have to make everything so dismal?"

"How do you think it feels?" said Kristian, 'How do you think it feels lying here like a corpse unable to help you or look after you! It feels like shit."

"You're proud, aren't you?" Emily said. "Has it never occurred to you that I've never in all my life had a chance to protect anyone else and make decisions and take responsibility for important things? Let me keep that. Don't take it away from me! All you have to do to help is keep me from being afraid." She found the matches and lit the candle. "The only thing that worries me is that they might come and take our food. Nothing else."

One day Kristian forgot to wind up his watch. At first he couldn't admit it, not right away, not till evening. Emily was standing at the sink; she stiffened but said nothing.

"I know," said Kristian. "It's unforgivable. My only duty and I've failed. Emily? Speak to me."

"they've all stopped," said Emily in a very low voice. "All the clocks have stopped. Now I'll never again know when it's time to go shopping."

He insisted, "It was unforgivable of me."

They said no more about it. But this business of the watch changed something; it established uncertainty, a reticence between them. Emily went out less often with her bags; the food shops were empty and going to the Erikssons' only made her sad. However, the last time she went there, she took the large Spanish silk shawl lying over the piano, thinking it might add a little colour to their barricaded window. On the way home she saw a dog. She tried to get it to come to her but it ran away.

When she came into the kitchen, she said, "I saw a dog."

Kristian was immediately interested. "Where? What did it look like?"

"A brown and white setter. Near the park. I called but it got scared and ran away. The rats aren't scared."

"Which way did it run?"

"Oh, it just ran off. Funny no one's eaten it yet. And what the poor dog must have been living on doesn't bear thinking about. In any case, it wasn't particularly thin."

Kristian lay down again. "Sometimes you astonish me," he said. "Women astonish me."

* * *

Their life went on unchanged. Kristian's leg got a little better, and now and then he managed to sit at the kitchen table. He'd sit there sorting the matches into piles and doing calculations: so many matches would last them such and such a length of time. Every time Emily came back from fetching water he would ask her if she had seen them. Then one morning she did see them.

"Were they men or women?"

"I don't know. They were a long way off in the park."

"Couldn't you see whether they were young or old?"

"No."

"I wonder," said Kristian, "I wonder if they've noticed too how it's getting darker all the time. I wonder what they think about. Do they try and talk things over and make plans, or are they just scared. Why haven't they gone away like all the others? And do they think they're entirely alone, that there isn't anyone else left, not a single..."

"Kris love, I don't know. I try not to think about them."

"But we have to think about them!" Kristian burst out. "Perhaps that's all there is, us and them. We could meet them."

"You can't mean that."

"On the contrary, I'm serious. We could talk to them. Figure out what we could do together. Share things."

"Not our food!" Emily shouted.

"Keep your cans and jars," said Kristian contemptuously. "We could share what's happened, the things you never want to talk about. What's happened, why it happened, and where we can go from here if there *is* any going on."

"I have to take the rubbish out," said Emily.

"You don't have to do any such thing. You need to listen to what I have to say. It's important." And Kristian went on talking, trying to communicate to her the conviction that had formed in him during all those days and weeks of being imprisoned in darkness. He offered Emily his respect for her judgment in exchange for the trust and loyalty he felt she owed him as his woman. In fact he was making her a declaration of love, but she didn't understand that, and left the room without a word so she wouldn't have to listen.

When she had gone Kristian was gripped by a terrible rage. He made his way to the window and tore down the Spanish shawl. Then he pried loose the boards one after another, attacking the window with a hatred born of disappointment till his leg gave way and he sank to his knees. But through a little opening at one side, daylight came into the room.

Emily had come back. She stood in the doorway and shouted, "You've torn my Spanish shawl!"

"Yes, I've torn your shawl. The world is coming to an end and little Emily's shawl is torn. What a shame! Give me the axe – now!"

Kristian threw himself at the barricade. Time and again he collapsed and had to lower the axe – and then he'd try again.

"Let me," whispered Emily.

"No. This has nothing to do with you."

But she moved forward to support him so he could continue. When the window was opened, she began sweeping up the mess he'd made. Kristian waited for her to speak but she said nothing. In the grey light from outside, their kitchen seemed unfamiliar, exposed, a room full of random shabbiness and unnecessary things.

Then Emily said, "They're coming," and without looking at him went on. "You seem to be doing pretty well on your leg. You're so difficult these days I can't cope with you. Come on, let's go out." She opened the kitchen door.

"But do you have confidence in me?" asked Kristian. "Do you believe in me?"

"Don't be so pompous – of course I do. But take your coat; it's getting colder." She helped him on with his coat and took his arm.

Outside it was already getting darker as evening came on. The others had come nearer. Very slowly, Kristian and Emily walked towards them.

The Forest

IN THOSE DAYS there was nothing but cow paths through the forest, which was so big that if you went looking for berries you could get lost and not find your way home again for days. We didn't dare go more than a little way in, and even then we would just stand there and listen to the silence for a while before running back. Matti was more scared than I was, but then he wasn't yet six years old. There was a drop-off below the hill, and Mum had given us quite a lecture about that hill before we said goodbye.

Mum worked in town so that we could spend our summer at the cottage, which she had rented through an advertisement. She had also hired Anna to make our meals. Mostly Anna just wanted to be left in peace. "Go out and play," she'd say.

Matti followed me everywhere, saying, "Wait for me!" and "What'll we play?" but he was way too little to hang out with. What are you supposed to do with a little brother? The days were really long.

Then, one very special day, Mum sent us a parcel and in the parcel was a book that changed everything – it was called *Tarzan of the Apes*.

Of course Matti couldn't read yet, but I would read him bits of it from time to time. Mostly though, I'd take Tarzan with me into a tree. Matti would stand at the bottom and pester me with questions. "What's happening now? Is Tarzan okay?"

Then Mum sent us *The Beasts of Tarzan* and *The Son of Tarzan*.

Anna said, "What a nice mum you boys have. It's such a shame you lost your poor papa."

"He's not lost!" Matti said. "He's big and strong and he's not afraid of anything, so you watch what you say about him!"

Later Matti announced that he was Tarzan's son.

The summer changed totally, and the biggest change was that we started going into the forest. We discovered that it was a jungle that no one had ever explored, and we ventured in farther and farther to where the trees crowded together in perpetual twilight. We had to learn to tread silently like Tarzan so as not to crack the smallest twig, and we learned to listen a new way. I explained that for the time being we couldn't use the cow paths, because the jungle beasts used them to reach their watering holes. I told Matti we had to be a bit careful with our wild friends, at least for now.

"All right, Tarzan," said Matti.

I taught him how to tell directions by the sun so we could find our way home, and I explained we must never set out in cloudy weather. My son became braver and more skilful, but he never quite overcame his fear of deadly ants.

Sometimes we lay on our backs in the moss, in some safe place, and gazed up into a mighty world of green. We hardly ever caught a glimpse of the sky, although the forest bore the sky on its roof. And though we could hear the wind moving through the treetops, the air was utterly still. There was never any danger because the jungle concealed and protected us.

One time we came to a stream. Tarzan's son knew the stream was full of piranhas, but he waded across it all the same – very quickly. I was proud of him, perhaps never more so than the time he ventured a little way into deep water, all by himself. I was standing behind a rock holding a safety line but he didn't know that.

I made us bows and arrows but we shot only one or two hyenas – we didn't really count them among our wild friends – and once a boa constrictor. We hit it right in the mouth and it died instantly.

When we came home to eat, Anna asked what we'd been playing and my son told her we were much too old to play. We were exploring the jungle.

"That's nice," said Anna. "You go right ahead. But do try not to be late for supper."

We discovered a new independence and followed only the Law of the Jungle, which can never be questioned and is strict and just. And the jungle opened its arms and accepted us. Each day, we had the heady experience of daring, of stretching our limits to the utmost, of being stronger than we'd dreamed. But we never killed anything smaller than ourselves.

August arrived with its black nights. When the sunset cast its red light between the tree trunks we would run home because we didn't want to see the darkness fall.

Then, when Anna had turned off the lamp and closed the kitchen door, we would lie in bed and listen. Something howled a long way off, then a hooting close to the cottage.

"Tarzan?" Matti whispered. "Did you hear that?"

"Sleep," I said. "Nothing can get in. Trust me, my son."

But suddenly I knew with a terrible certainty that my wild friends were friends no longer. I caught the rank smell of wild beasts rubbing their hairy bodies against the wall of the cottage... It was I who had conjured them, and only I could send them away before it was too late.

"Papa!" Matti cried. "They're coming in!"

"Don't be silly," I said. "It's only some old owls and foxes making a noise; now go to sleep. All that stuff about the jungle was something we made up. It isn't true."

I said it very loud so they would hear outside.

"Of course it's true," Matti shrieked. "You're wrong! They're real!" He worked himself up into a real state.

The next summer Matti wanted us to go into the jungle again. But to be honest, that would just have been leading him on.

The PE Teacher's Death

ONE SPRING, WHEN THE TREES in the Cambrai district were about to turn green, something tragic happened that had a lengthy and profound effect on the Southern Latin Boys' School: the PE teacher hanged himself in the gym. The caretaker found him on Saturday evening. Gym was replaced till further notice by drawing lessons for the lower classes, and almost without exception the boys chose extremely morbid themes for their sketches.

The school was closed on the day of the funeral. In the headmaster's view, the sad event might have had something to do with the teacher failing to pass an exam required for the job of Director of Physical Education, but there were other theories too. One set of speculations concerned a copse of trees a kilometre west of the school that was due to be cleared. This little patch of woodland was barely three acres in size. The PE teacher had been in the habit of taking his pupils there on Sundays. It was believed that he was the one who had cut the barbed-wire fence that the Highrise Development Company had placed around the site to stop people climbing into the wood and getting into mischief before it was cut down. Whatever the truth of the matter, it was generally considered that his death had at the very least been an overreaction and entirely unnecessary.

On the day of the funeral Henri Pivot and his wife Florence, known as Flo, drove out of the town; they had been invited to dinner with a business colleague of Henri's in the building trade. The traffic was moving very slowly and occasionally stood still for long periods. They had a two-hour drive ahead of them.

When Flo was in a bad mood, her face grew narrower and her eyes seemed to enlarge and turn steeply down at the temples. Henri used to tease her about her dramatic mosaic eyes. Her tightly permed hair would also have suited a mosaic, but not her glasses. As for Henri, nature had given him what you might call a pleasant manly appearance, one that inspired confidence, although truthfully his features were neither well defined nor particularly memorable.

"Stuck again," said Flo. "How I hate sitting in traffic jams; it's so humiliating. You feel so confined. I'd never dream of asking people from another city to drive over for dinner. We could have gone to the funeral instead."

Henri said, "But you thought we didn't need to go."

"Need and need. I say a lot of things. And why didn't she invite the boys as well – it's not as if they don't eat! Did she forget we have children?"

"But they wanted to play football. They wouldn't have wanted to go to Nicole's dinner party."

"Henri, you know how it works. X invites Y so Y can say sorry, can't come, and everybody's happy."

The queue of cars began moving again. After a while he said, "You don't like her."

"We've only met once. At the Chatains. I've no particular feelings about her."

The landscape around them was flat and featureless apart from recurring groups of high-rise blocks set at an angle to the road, and petrol stations, all the ordinary roadside places, all the same, without character, monotonous as polite conversation.

"Henri."

"Yes, darling?"

"I was just thinking about it..."

"I know. Did the boys say anything – did they ask?"

"No."

"But they do know, don't they?"

"Poor sweet Henri, the whole school knows. This is a horrible place. Where are their houses?"

"They haven't started construction yet; this is a clearance."

"A clearance?"

"They've cut down the trees; it's a clearance." He knew at once this wasn't a good answer and waited, resigned, for what she would say about trees and for his own explanation that if homes had to be built and so forth, and how people are more important than trees and how there may be too many of them but they still need places to live.

But Flo said nothing. She polished her glasses on a corner of her dress and it wasn't until they'd gone several more miles that she repeated that nevertheless they should have gone to the funeral.

"We don't know his people," Henri retorted. "No one would have cared if we were there or not."

"Henri. I don't feel well."

"But we can't just stop right here. Is it really bad? You don't usually get carsick."

"Did you bring the cognac?"

"It's in the glove compartment."

The desolate landscape continued.

"You know what?" said Flo. "This dinner party is ab-so-lutely unnecessary."

Henri forced himself to be patient. "You're wrong. It's not unnecessary. When I'm working with Michel and they ask us to dinner, then we have to go. You know that."

"Yes, of course, sorry, sorry. You're just building your buildings."

"Flo, please. Make the effort to be nice this evening. It's important to me."

"Of course. I know. I'll try."

"Feeling better now?"

"Maybe a bit."

"Flo darling, don't think about that business with the, I mean... It's too bad, but that sort of thing happens all the time. People are weak, they can't cope, they give up. And the world goes on. You know life goes on, just the same. And in a week or two there'll be a new PE teacher."

She swung round suddenly to face her husband's calm profile, to face everything he seemed to her to symbolise right then, and she burst out, "Nothing will ever be the same! And he wasn't weak. On the contrary, he was so strong he couldn't take it any more! And we did nothing to help him!"

They had finally reached an area of expensive bunga-lows on the outskirts of the city, and climbed out of the car. Henri took the flowers and Flo's coat and said, "Now, we'll do our best, allright? Then we can go home again and you can sleep as late as you like tomorrow morning."

The house where Nicole and Michel lived was an architectural masterpiece, an exquisite jewel, all its details in perfect harmony. It reminded Flo of the sort of gallery opening you can't leave for fear that the artist will see you sneaking off. Nicole herself was like her house: big and beautiful and in some sense removed.

"Florence, darling," she said, "I'm so glad Henri brought you. Unfortunately Michel won't be here till a bit later. He promised to phone. These endless, awful conferences!"

"Don't I know it," said Henri. "Business first! What a beautiful table you've set, Nicole. Perfect."

At the end of the meal Henri raised his glass, and with his natural ease of manner he thanked their hostess and called her a jewel in a perfect setting, alluding with humour and elegance to fishing trips he'd been on with Michel in the good old days, adding an entirely new anecdote about the construction business and finishing with a poetic allusion to the coming spring.

"Thank you so much, dear friends," said Nicole. "Thank you, thank you. I can only say how lovely it is to have you here. And now let's have a cup of coffee and a little cognac in the living room. I can't wait to hear what Florence will have to say about the decor. Wait a minute, just one second. Let me switch on the spotlight."

"Henri," whispered Flo. "Is it okay so far? Not being too quiet, am I?"

"Fine. Everything's fine. Just don't forget, darling – this is very important to me."

She drew away from his arm and said, "I know, I know, really important. You're putting up big buildings."

Nicole came back and explained that the garden outside should be illuminated better but the lighting hadn't been properly arranged yet. They mustn't let it bother them if it came into the room.

Flo asked, "What's coming into the room? When is it coming?"

"So lovely, so absolutely lovely," said Henri. "You've done so much since the last time I was here!"

A square of lawn could be seen through a glass panel, lit by bright Bengal light and enclosed by a wall.

"Henri," whispered Flo. "They're in your pocket..."

He handed her her dark glasses.

Nicole was talking about Monsieur Deschamps and his design artistry, at once original and restrained, expensive but perfect. "Nothing extraneous, everything clean, bare, and balanced. See how the violet and leaf-brown of the lilacs is repeated in the background? Clever, don't you think? Especially the wilted flowers."

Flo suddenly found she was having difficulty focusing, and her hostess spoke so very fast, she found it hard to follow what she was saying. She asked carefully, "But why dead flowers? What is it that repeats?"

Nicole laughed her high, light laugh. "Dead flowers? But darling, so you'll believe it's a real plant! Cognac?"

"Not for me, thanks. I have the car."

"Florence? Just a tiny one?"

"Thanks very much. It doesn't need to be tiny." Flo added slowly, "I don't quite understand..."

Henri cut in. "What a pity Michel couldn't be here."

"Yes, isn't it? But he promised to try. God, how sick I am of all these conferences! Conferences, conferences, conferences..."

"Absolutely, Nicole. I know what it's like. But Michel's very responsible."

Flo said again, "If only I could understand why. Why he did it..."

"Flo," Henri warned, but she went on excitedly. "Why? No one hangs himself for no reason!" She emptied her glass and stared straight at Nicole.

Nicole lifted her shoulders. After a quick glance at Henri, she looked away.

"I'm sorry, but I need to talk about it. We have to try and understand what happened to him, don't we? What he meant by all the things he said that time we wouldn't listen. Henri. We didn't listen, and it was important!"

Nicole drew a deep breath and said, "He was the boys' PE teacher, I believe? I heard about it. Such a sad story. But you didn't know him all that well, did you?"

Flo wasn't listening. She was looking down, trying to remember. "It was something important about how everything passes us by because we don't... No, wait a minute. He believed that as long as we're alive we ought to... That suddenly it's too late? Henri? What was it that was so important?"

Henri turned to Nicole and hurriedly explained: "He was going round with one of those protest petitions, you know the sort of thing. And he wanted the parents to sign it."

"Oh, one of those."

Flo sat up straight and exclaimed, "And we didn't sign it!"

"Florence, darling, you have to watch out for that kind of thing. You never know. They never say exactly what they mean, and then you're trapped. That's something Michel and I understand better than most. It can be about politics."

"No. It was about trees. Some woods."

"Flo, love, it had nothing to do with that."

The telephone rang and Nicole ran to answer it. While she was away Flo asked, "You mean about him hanging himself?"

"Flo, for heaven's sake, let it go. This isn't the time."

Their hostess came back. "Wrong number. I thought it might be Michel. But you haven't finished your coffee. It must be cold; let me top it up."

"Coffee!" Henri exclaimed. "Why don't people have Thermoses these days? I remember how much fun it was in the old days when Michel and I used to go fishing..."

Flo repeated, "What do you mean that had nothing to do with it?"

"It didn't. Believe me, it didn't. It had nothing to do with the woods."

Nicole opened the glass doors to the garden. A light rain had begun to fall. She paused a moment on the threshold to breathe the mild, damp night air. If only Michel would come home and help her; if only his business connections didn't always have wives. Big beautiful Nicole wished passionately that the world of calm and charm she'd created might be left in peace, that her life might as far as possible be left undisturbed by all the ugliness and chaos that crowded the world outside. Why couldn't they talk about something nice? It would be so easy!

"Woods," she said, surreptitiously pushing the carafe of cognac a little farther away. "I've always been fascinated by woodlands. Michel and I once had a whole week to ourselves in Denmark. Those incredible beech forests! It was springtime then, too. Absolutely incredible. Henri, a cigar?"

"No thanks, but look at that – the same brand Michel and I used to smoke!"

They smiled at each other.

"You know what?" said Flo. "I love the smell of cigars. It makes everything feel so leisurely."

"So true," Nicole blurted out in relief. "Not at all like cigarettes! A little mineral water?"

"No, thanks." Flo looked at her beautiful hostess, who suddenly seemed so friendly and straightforward. She touched her hand almost shyly and confided, "Nicole, maybe you'll understand; I think about it all the time. It's as if we'd hurt him by not signing that petition."

The phone rang and it was another wrong number. Nicole was visibly annoyed when she came back. "Florence, dear, what difference could it possibly have made?" she said. "Except it might have eased your conscience. Anyway, did you ever think how pretentious it is to feel guilty? I read somewhere that when people die we always have a guilty conscience whether we've been nice to them or not. It's just the way it is and absolutely nothing to worry about. Did your sons have a guilty conscience? Of course not. They probably went out and played football or something."

Complete silence.

"Hang on," said Henri. "Both of you, listen to me. His students went and cut the barbed wire in lots of places. Our boys did it too."

"Oh, did they really!" Flo exclaimed. "How wonderful! But how did they manage it?"

"With wire-cutters, I suppose. I thought that might make you feel better."

Flo laughed. "There, Nicole dear – you see they did take the matter seriously! Now that was a real mark of respect, don't you think? They didn't just shrug their shoulders and dismiss the whole thing as some sad story!"

Nicole turned slowly red. "There was talk of some sort of exam," she said. "Is it possible they actually take exams? Ordinary gym teachers? And then he failed it and was so upset he... my God. What was the exam?"

Henri said very abruptly, "Climbing a rope. To qualify for the permanent staff."

"And he couldn't do it?"

"No. He tried year after year."

"So he went and hanged himself. With the rope? Was he too old? Or too fat?"

Flo got up from the table. "He was the only person I've ever met who took what he wanted to do and was trying to do so seriously that he was ready to die for it! And no one helped him!"

Nicole, now really cross, spat out, "For goodness' sake, he had to climb it by himself!"

"Nicole," said Henri in warning.

There was a moment of silence; all they could hear was traffic hissing past outside the wall. Flo sat down again.

"Florence," said Nicole. "I know you've had a bad experience. I understand that, believe me. But would it have been such a comfort to him if you had signed his petition? Think about it."

"I don't know. Maybe I'm the one who needed comforting... But I didn't listen to him. He said something about us being unhappy and not even knowing it, so nothing could be done... He said it all could have been so simple. Henri? What was it that was so simple? Was it something about nature?"

"Flo, don't you think we ought to be getting home?"

"That green wave was over and done with ages ago," Nicole began, but Flo interrupted her vehemently.

"Green, you say? What do you know about green? There isn't a colour in this house that I'd call green. Even the grass isn't a proper green; it's all just horrible decorator colours that are tasteful! No, don't say it, I know I'm behaving badly. Where are my glasses? No, the other ones, the ones I was wearing when we came."

Henri handed her her glasses and said, "Nicole, I really think we'll be on our way."

"Must you really? I thought maybe a little snack before you go..."

"Another time. And we've the boys to think of."

"Of course, naturally. How are they doing anyway?"

"Fine. Just fine."

"Nicole," said Flo. "I've been awful, I know I have. Unforgivable. But perhaps you'd understand if you'd met him. He was somehow so innocent. So wide awake. Fully awake to everything, and brave enough to dare. And now I wonder – how can any of us ever accomplish anything if not even someone like him..."

"Florence darling, of course you're upset. I mean, it's easy getting people all worried and anxious, playing Tarzan out in the woods and saying how terribly simple and happy the world could be and then hanging yourself just because you can't climb a rope! He was deceiving himself and everyone else, it seems to me. And this thing about being unhappy and not knowing it – what a thing to say! You can't be unhappy and not know it!"

"Of course you can!" Flo shouted. "And he didn't deceive anybody. It was us who let him down!" She reached for the cognac and filled her glass; I wish something mattered to me so much that I was ready to die for it!" She walked out through the glass doors.

The phone rang. Henri waited; he was very tired. Nicole came back. "This time it was Michel. He said hello and he'll be here as soon as he can. Surely you can stay a bit longer? Just a little late evening snack? He'll be so disappointed…"

"I'm sorry, Nicole, but we really must go."

They both looked out into the garden. Flo was nowhere to be seen.

Henri said, "Well, maybe we can wait a little."

"I don't think it did rain," Nicole said. "We're planning a small piece of sculpture out there. A faun or a boy holding a fish."

"I think the fish."

"Do you? It goes in the middle. We cleared away the bushes because they looked so untidy. I mean, you can't live in a jungle, now, can you?"

"No," said Henri.

"There was a tree just outside the wall that put the whole coffee area in the shade."

"Of course," said Henri. "Shall we go out and get a little air?"

Flo wasn't feeling well. There was something wrong with her glasses and the walls that surrounded the square of lawn seemed totally unreal – as if they were closing in on her from all sides. They were topped with shards of glass all the way round. She dropped her glass on the brick floor near the barbecue.

"Nicole! Here's some more broken glass for your wall. What an ugly, ugly wall." She walked right up to Nicole and went on. "What would you say if someone, just some person, sailed over your wall in one great leap, just soared over it, someone a hundred times wiser and warmer than us, someone who just came from nowhere, as free and light as a feather, and stood right here, and saw right through everything, and knew?"

Nicole answered in a low, merciless voice, "On a liana, I suppose. Or maybe on a rope? It's a little hard to grasp exactly what you're getting at, dear little Florence, it's all so ethereal, but is it Tarzan you're referring to, or some kind of Jesus, or could it possibly be your wonderful PE teacher?"

"Yes!" cried Flo. "All of the above! But if he did come, you'd not know him or take him in. I know that." She threw herself headlong onto the grass with her face on her arms.

Henri said, "Nicole, I'm sorry."

"Don't be. I forget so easily. Couldn't you stay over in the guestroom? It would be no trouble at all."

"Thanks very much, but we really have to get home."

"She can't just lie there on the ground like that; the grass is all wet..."

"Let her sleep." He cautiously put his hands on Nicole's shoulders and said, "Nicole, you're the best wife Michel could ever have had. You're good for each other. Flo and I are good for each other, too. Let's just sit here a moment and not say a word. No, don't say anything. In silence."

They sat on the chairs near the barbecue. It was an uncommonly warm night for early spring. All they could hear were the cars going by. Nicole leaned back in her chair and closed her eyes. "You know, Henri, I think it's kind of horrible when it's completely quiet at night."

"You do?"

"Yes. Kind of awful. Menacing. We have people here all the time, Michel knows so many people, but when they've gone home and he's gone to sleep, all I can hear, almost all night, are the cars driving by. There are several hours when there aren't even any cars. You know, total silence."

Henri lit one of Michel's cigars.

She went on, "That tree outside the wall, the one that blocked the sun."

"Yes, the tree."

"A boy climbed it one day. Our neighbours had sent him to ask us if our drains were also backing up. And, instead of ringing the bell, he used a rope to get over the wall."

Henri said, "Playing Tarzan, I suppose..." then cut himself short. "Did he go back the same way?"

"I didn't see."

Flo sat up on the lawn and asked, "And were your drains backing up? No? Nicole, it's been a lovely evening. I forgive us. I forgive you. We're all forgiven." She got up and went into the house.

"Nicole...," Henri said. He was searching for words, and she immediately came to his aid. "Don't thank me! Such fun having you here. Come again sometime when Michel is home. Have you got everything? Not leaving anything behind?" Her great blue eyes were as beautiful as ever, showing no trace of displeasure. She added, "You know, Henri dear, it's so easy to forget."

In the car Flo fell asleep. After an hour, she woke up and said, "Should I write her a letter?"

"No, I don't think so. It's a bad idea to bother people who easily forget."

"You're not angry? You'll never be able to take me there again."

"Of course I will. And the sooner, the better."

She looked at him for a while, then went back to staring straight ahead. It was beginning to rain. The asphalt was gleaming, and the scent of wet grass came to them through the half-open car window.

After a while Henri told her about a tree he'd climbed when he was little, and how, unable to get down again, he'd stayed up there all day.

"I was terrified," he said. "Mostly I was afraid of being laughed at."

"And they came and rescued you?"

"No. I climbed down by myself. In tears, I was so scared. And then climbed right back up again."

"Yes," said Flo. "I understand."

There were not many cars on the road now at night. Henri imagined Nicole lying listening to them pass one by one, feeling more and more isolated. A magnificent woman, he thought to himself. Probably easy to live with. I have a difficult woman. It's all fine.

As they approached the city where they had their home, he said, almost in passing, "That thing about being unhappy and not knowing it?"

"Maybe it's not so bad," Flo said. "I don't think it's so bad if you do know it."

The boys had gone to bed. Henri set the alarm clock and collected the papers he needed for the next day's work. Flo's dress was stained with earth and grass, so she put it to soak in the bathtub.

The Gulls

Now he had ripped all the luggage open again, for the third time.

"But Arne, darling," said Elsa. "We'll never get going if you don't start trusting the lists. We've been making them for weeks."

"I know, I know, stop going on about it. I just have to check one or two little things." His thin face was clenched with anxiety, and his hands had started shaking again.

He's going to get better.

"He's going to be fine," the doctor had said. "A month's peace and quiet is all he needs. He's overworked; it's the school's fault."

"What time is it, Elsa? Do you think it's too late to call the headmaster? Just to make sure he understands clearly, really clearly. I mean, so I can explain in detail."

"No. Don't phone again; it's not necessary. Don't even think about it."

But of course he does think about it, all the time. The school understood a long time ago that his resignation wasn't to be taken seriously. They understood that, and they want him back as soon as he's well again.

Arne turned to his wife with the weary intensity of repetition. "Bloody school. Bloody kids."

She said, "You ought to be working with much older students. They're too young, they don't know any better. You just have to understand..."

"Oh really? Understand them? All you need to understand is that they're hellish little wild beasts who will stop at nothing, nothing, I tell you, to destroy my work and make my life a living hell."

"Stop it, Arne! Calm down!"

"Right. Calm down. Wonderful. Nothing makes me feel less like calming down than someone telling me to calm down!"

Elsa started laughing. Her tension simply dissolved in a huge laugh, a laugh that suddenly made her beautiful.

"You idiot!" he shouted. "You stupid woman!" In a rage, he emptied his bag out onto the floor, turned his back on it and covered his face with his hands.

Elsa said very quietly, "I'm sorry. Come here."

He went to where she was sitting and, with his head in her arms, he said, "Tell me again how it's going to be."

"We come closer and closer. Papa's boat is small but very sturdy. We're on our honeymoon. You're sitting in the bow and you've never been in the islands before. With every new skerry, you think we're there, but no, we're going all the way out, right out to an island that's hardly a shadow on the horizon. And when we land, it won't be Papa's island any more, it'll be ours, for weeks and weeks, and the city and everyone in it will fade away, till in the end they won't even exist or have any hold on us at all. Just pure peace and quiet. And now in the spring the days and nights can be windless, soundless, somehow transparent... No boats will go by for days at a time."

She stopped. He said, "And then?"

"We won't need to work. No translating. No post, no telephone. No demands. We'll hardly even open our books. We won't fish or plant anything. We'll just wait till we find something we want to do, and if we don't find anything we want to do, well, that won't matter, either."

"But what if we do want to do something?"

He always asked that question and she always answered, "Then we'll play. We'll play at something totally silly."

"Like what? What do you play on the island?"

She laughed and said, "With the birds."

He sat up and looked at her.

"Yes, with the birds, the seabirds. I collect dry bread for them all winter. And when I come out in the spring, all I have to do is whistle and they know me. There are white wings everywhere; they take the bread right out of my hands in full flight! The loveliest game you can imagine."

They both stood up. Elsa raised her arms to show how the big gull came to her, and then she told him how it felt when its wing softly brushed her cheek and when its cold, flat, gull feet trustingly landed on her hand. She was no longer talking to him but to herself, talking about her own gull, the one who came back each spring and tapped at her window with its beak; the gull she called Casimir.

"What a name," said Arne.

"Yes, isn't it?" Elsa threw her arms round him and looked up into his face. "What do you think? Shall we go to bed?"

"Yes, but you know what a restless sleeper I am these days. I don't want to keep you awake. Fruit juice or water?"

"Water," said Elsa.

* * *

It was evening when they finally set out. A warm sunset still lingered over sea and sky. It was dead calm and indescribably beautiful. The large islands were soon behind them, and only very low skerries marked an invisible horizon. Arne was sitting in the bow. From time to time he'd turn and they'd smile at each other. She drew his attention to a long flight of migratory birds going past on their way north, and she pointed out several long-tailed ducks, their wings beating at lightning speed close above their reflections in the water. "The welcoming committee!" she shouted, but he couldn't hear her over the motor.

When they arrived, a screaming cloud of hundreds of seabirds rose chalk-white against the evening sky. Arne stood looking up at the circling birds, the painter in his hand.

"They'll settle down," said Elsa. "But you see, they're nesting right now. We just need to watch out for the nests right next to the cottage."

They secured the boat and carried up their bags, and she gave him the key to unlock the house. Inside was a single low room with four windows. A damp chill had settled in it. All four windows looked out on a sea with no horizon.

"It's totally unreal," said Arne. "Like being on the top of a mountain or maybe up in a balloon. I think I can sleep tonight. Shall we leave the unpacking till morning? We don't need lamps, do we? What about lighting a fire?"

"We don't need anything," said Elsa. "Everything's fine."

* * *

The birds started screeching before dawn, like a thousand furies spoiling for war. Their feet tramped over the sheet-metal roof as if laying siege to the cottage. They were everywhere.

Arne woke Elsa. "What's the matter with them?" he said.

"They're always like that in the morning," she said. "One starts screeching and all the others start. They'll soon quiet down. Let's go back to sleep." She took his hand in hers and fell asleep again at once. The birds went on screeching. He tried to ignore it, but he could feel his old fear creeping closer, his horror of noise, of anything out of control. Then he found refuge in the memory of last night's proud fulfilment, in a renewed longing to shelter and protect, and so the clamour of the birds lost importance.

The sun rose, drowning the whole room in strong pink and orange light. Outside the cottage it was quiet.

I'll learn to be calm, he thought. I'll learn.

* * *

They drank their morning coffee.

Suddenly there was tapping at the window. Elsa leaped up and exclaimed, "It's Casimir! He's back!"

An enormous herring gull was pressed against the window pane. It looked impatient.

"Is there any more coffee?" Arne said.

"I'll warm it up. Just a minute..." Elsa quickly put some dry bread to soak, cut a piece of cheese rind into convenient little bits, and carried it all out to the front steps. She whistled her birdcall, raised the dish with her beautiful round arms, and Casimir came and stood on her hand while he ate. "Look at that!" she called. "He remembers me!"

Arne asked, "How long do they live?"

"Forty years, if they're lucky."

"And they always come back?"

"Always."

* * *

Arne was the first to see the eider. She was sitting on her nest under a bush by the steps, almost indistinguishable against the grey-brown spring soil.

"A good omen," said Elsa earnestly. "And she didn't fly away even when we came near. Now she'll stay till her chicks hatch. Isn't that lovely?"

Arne studied the eider, fascinated. To him the bird's long face seemed full of patience and wisdom. She sat completely still.

He said, "I've never seen an eider before. I'll sit here on the steps for a bit."

"You do that, darling. I'll unpack."

Arne sat a long time watching the motionless bird, a clever bird that knew she had nothing to fear.

Very slowly he walked past her and further up across the island. But as he neared the navigation marker at the high end, he was attacked. A raging swarm of howling birds dive-bombed him, again and again, purposefully and maliciously, like Stukas. He screamed back at them and waved his arms in panic. He felt their wings beating on his head and suddenly he was bitten, a wicked little nip. He cowered on the granite with his arms over his face shouting, "Elsa! Elsa!"

She came running and shouting at the same time, "It's their nests! There are a lot of nests on this side. I should have warned you."

They went back down to the cottage, and he flung himself on the bed and stared at the wall.

"I'm so sorry," said Elsa. "They're very aggressive at this time of year and there are too many of them. And if you stand up to them it makes it worse..."

"Don't I know it. Too many children in every class, in every bloody class. And if you stand up to them, it just makes it worse. Don't say it. I'm going to sleep."

* * *

Towards evening he went out to have a look at the eider. Two gulls were giving a strange performance on the rock slope nearby. With a rapid series of short sharp cries and powerfully flapping wings, the cock besieged his hen.

Arne went back inside. "It's bestial," he said. "It's disgusting."

"Do you think so? I think it's beautiful. Shall we have vegetable soup today or would you rather have chicken?"

"Whichever you like. I don't care."

* * *

Elsa lay awake listening to the cries of the long-tailed ducks. She would have enjoyed telling him about the long-tailed ducks, those mysterious birds, and getting him to listen for their seductive calls far out at sea, but after the incident with the terns she didn't dare talk about birds. His hands had started to shake again and for several days he wouldn't leave the house. He'd only go as far as the steps, where he would sit and watch the eider. Once he said, "She seems so content with everything, doesn't she?" And he asked when the chicks would hatch.

Casimir had become a problem for Elsa. The tapping at the window had to stop. She moved the box he liked to stand on and hid his food dish. But wherever she went, the huge bird followed her with his plaintive, ingratiating chirping. Arne watched and made sarcastic remarks. In the end she practically stopped going out. It was only while Arne was reading or asleep that she rushed through her outdoor chores, threw Casimir's food on the granite slope, and sneaked back into the house. They had become excessively cautious with each other and talked only about safe everyday trivia.

Then one night the wind changed and began to blow from the northeast. The shift in the wind woke Elsa, and she went to the window to check on the boat.

"Arne," she said, "the boat's pulling at her moorings."

Down by the shore she was careful to explain what needed to be done. He took time over it and fixed the lines quite passably. The birds were silent.

In the morning Arne was in a better mood than she'd seen him in for quite some time. Thank God, he was finally cheerful. As usual he went to look at the eider, who was sleeping under her rosebush.

"She's asleep," he whispered. "When the leaves open, she'll feel more protected. Don't you think?"

"Oh yes," said Elsa. "She'll be just fine, then. Why don't we go for a walk along the shore and look for firewood? We're out of kindling and I can't get the big pieces to burn without it."

"I can fix that," said Arne. "I'll go and chop you some kindling. Easy, it'll take no time at all."

She let him go, forgetting about the gull that nested beside the woodpile every year. When she finally remembered and rushed out to call him back, it was too late. She met him coming back with the axe dangling from his hand. He threw himself down on the bed and said, "There were three eggs."

"What do you mean?"

"Three eggs. Three birds. I threw them in the water. Plus the nest." He was silent a moment, then said, "The nest floated away. But the eggs sank like stones, straight to the bottom."

Elsa stood and stared at his dismissive back. She didn't want to tell him that if you take away a seabird's nest and eggs, she'll just build a new nest and lay new eggs in exactly the same place. She went down to the woodpile, found the crime scene, filled the place with stones, then waited behind the shed till the gull came back. The bird examined the stones, tried to cover them with her body, got up again, walked round, sat still for a while, tried again, then began collecting dry grass in her beak and stuffing it clumsily between the stones.

"You idiot," Elsa whispered. "You damned, stupid idiot..." She wanted to weep, and suddenly she was sick and tired of Arne and all his imaginary terrors, his pretentious sensitivities. She ran to the cottage and sat on the edge of his bed and gave him a detailed and somewhat cruel account of the gull searching for her eggs.

He listened in silence and then when she had finished he turned and lay on his back and just looked at her. Then he smiled. "So what shall we play at now? Try to scare each other? Hunt for eggs? It was you who said we should find some silly game to play."

Elsa got up, went to the kitchen counter, angrily prepared Casimir's food dish, threw open the door and whistled.

Arne shouted, "You'll disturb the eider! Can't you feed that damned gull on the other side of the house!"

Casimir came. The same persistent piercing cry, the same strong soft wings touching her face, the same firm grip on her hand. She laughed out loud, let the dish fall, and grabbed the gull with both hands, overcoming the powerful resistance of his wings. It was just exactly as she had imagined it, a great silken-smooth life force caught and held in her hands. To her astonishment, the rare, furious joy of clasping the creature in her arms suddenly went right through her and took her breath away – and at that moment the huge bird twisted out of her grasp, soared out over the shore and vanished. It was very quiet. Elsa stood where she was without turning round.

Arne said, "I was watching." His voice was distant and dry.

It was a mild, overcast day, the sort of hesitant weather when nothing seems to move. The leaves of the rosebush were on the point of opening, wrinkled and light green. Arne didn't look at the eider but he knew she was still there, an honourable companion.

They probably should have brought a radio with them but they'd finally decided on a long, blessed silence. That had been the plan. Towards evening a thick mist rolled in from the sea, bringing an even deeper silence. In an instant the island became unreal, diminished, as if the cottage's four windows had blinders of thick white wool. Ideal conditions for the eider to take her chicks down to the water.

Elsa made their evening tea. They drank it while reading their books. After tea, Arne went out on the steps – at just the right moment. The eider was making her way slowly down the slope, her chicks in a line behind her. It was unbelievable, fantastic, such a remark-able thing to see that he called to Elsa so she could see it too. And at that moment came a powerful beating of wings and a great white bird dived out of the sky and seized one of the chicks. As Arne watched in helpless horror, the eider chick disappeared down the bird's throat bit by bit. He screamed, rushed forward, picked up a stone and threw it. Never before in his life had Arne thrown anything straight and true, but he did so now. The bird fell on the granite slope, wings outspread like an open flower, whiter than the mist, with the legs of the eider chick still sticking out of its mouth.

"Elsa, I'll kill you!" he cried.

She was standing beside him. She touched his arm lightly and said, "Look, they're marching along undis-turbed."

The eider and her remaining chicks were heading on down to the water where they disappeared into the mist.

He turned to her. "Don't you see what's happened? I've killed Casimir. I attacked him, took him out!" Wildly excited, he lifted the dead bird by one wing and walked down towards the water to throw it into the sea. Elsa stood and watched him go. She decided to remain silent and not tell him that this wasn't Casimir, or even a herring gull that he was consigning to the deep. And that, of course, her own gull would never come back.

The Hothouse

WHEN UNCLE WAS REALLY OLD he developed an interest in botany. He'd never married, but his large and benevolent extended family always took good care of him. Now his relatives bought him expensive and beautifully illustrated books on botany. Uncle praised the books and set them aside.

But when they'd all gone off to their jobs and their schools and whatever else they were busy with, he would go out and take the tram to the Botanical Gardens. It was a laborious and always unpleasantly chilly journey, but the awkwardness of the enterprise was more than compensated by anticipation, and by the crucial moment when he opened the door to the Hothouse and was met by the warmth and the gentle but powerful scent of the flowers. And the silence. There was rarely anyone there.

Uncle would put off looking at the waterlily pond, that always had to come last. He would wander down the narrow passages through tropical greenery. The jungle brushed past him but he never deliberately touched the plants and did not read their names. Just occasionally he felt an irrational desire to walk straight into the flowering luxuriance in frank adoration, to feel it rather than just look at it. This dangerous desire became even stronger when he came near the waterlily, the lotus pond, a shallow pool whose clear water bubbled forth in a constant babbling stream – what would it be like to take off his shoes, roll up his trousers and stride in, wading among the broad-leaved flowers, letting them glide past him and come together again behind him as though nothing had happened? Entirely alone; warm and alone in the Hothouse.

Near the water was a little wrought-iron bench, painted white, where Uncle liked to rest his legs and lose himself in a kind of contemplation and reflection that gradually freed him from all the concerns of the world outside.

High above the pond rose a glass cupola, constructed so long ago that it was really beautiful to look at. The bridge beneath the cupola was a delicate tracery of light, fin-de-siècle, metal arabesques, and the spiral staircase up to it had the same playfully seductive elegance. Sometimes people clunked up the spiral staircase and crossed the bridge quickly before coming down again and disappearing; they were always in a hurry and hardly ever gave the lily pond a glance.

Donkeys, thought Uncle. Strong legs but no brains.

The caretaker would sit behind a large luxuriant bush, either reading the paper or crocheting. Uncle was several times on the verge of asking him what all that crocheting was for, but he let it go, preferring the restful detachment of silence. But they would acknowledge each other's presence with a little nod of the head.

Sometimes the caretaker would leave his bush and pass the lily pond on some errand. Once he happened to pass when Uncle was on his way home and hurried forward to hold the heavy door. Uncle's relatives were not allowed to open doors for him at home, but in this case it was such an obvious gesture of respect that he was able to accept it. He was the Grand Old Man of the Hothouse, the only person who understood.

One day when Uncle came he found his bench already occupied by an old gentleman with a velvet collar and a drooping moustache. Uncle walked on through the green corridors and when he felt tired came back to the pond, but the bench was still occupied. It was a very small bench with barely room for two. After waiting a little he went home.

Next time the same man was sitting on Uncle's bench, and now he had a book. He didn't even glance at the waterlilies, he just read. Uncle was so annoyed that he went to the caretaker and spoke to him for the first time ever. "Who's that? Does he come here often?"

"Oh yes," said the caretaker. "Recently he's been coming every day. I'm so sorry."

And so it went. Every time Uncle came to the Hothouse, he would find the old man sitting there – right in the middle of the bench, what's more. But even if he'd made room for Uncle they would have been forced to sit uncomfortably close together, and it would have been idiotic to sit like that without exchanging a word, so they'd probably be drawn into conversation. This individual was bound to be a talkative type, and he looked so extremely old that there could be no doubt he must be very lonely.

The caretaker brought Uncle a chair but he didn't want it and just stood waiting behind a palm while his legs grew more and more tired. The intruder never once got up to have a look round; he just sat as if glued to the bench, reading, ridiculous little round glasses on his nose. Uncle would wait until the last possible moment before his relatives returned from work, then catch the tram home in rage and disappointment.

One day it was even worse. When it was time to go home, the old man got up to leave at exactly the same moment; the bench was now free but it was too late. Uncle tried to escape but the other was surprisingly quick on his legs and both gentlemen reached the double door of the main entrance at the same time. And the old devil held the door open for Uncle and stood and waited! An insufferable, humiliating situation. Neither moved or spoke. Uncle had decided not to say a single word to this interloper.

It was the caretaker who saved the day. Being a wise man who had grown rather tired of plants, he sometimes took an interest in his few visitors and their concerns. Now he hurried over, politely opened the other half of the door and bowed. The two visitors passed out side by side and turned firmly in opposite directions. This forced Uncle to make a long detour to his tram. And next day the old devil was there again, sitting reading in the middle of the bench.

The problem of the bench became almost an obsession. Uncle began to see the other man as a personal enemy. At night he would lie awake and wonder whether this man was older or younger than himself, if he had relations who looked after him, whether he actively disliked flowers and only sought the warmth, what it was he was always reading, whether his enormous moustache was intended as some kind of challenge...

Finally one fine winter's day the bench was empty again. Uncle sat down quickly and gazed at the lily pond, so long absent from his meditations. But his sense of peace was gone; he could think of nothing but the other man, the trespasser. And then the door opened and in he came. His stick tapped steadily on the floor all the way to the bench, then struck the floor twice, hard. "You're sitting on my bench."

It would have been childish to say, "No, it's mine." He must be neither hostile nor submissive. After a desperate search for words he finally said, "My dear sir, I'm as deaf as a post."

His enemy sighed, it seemed with relief, found room beside Uncle and opened his book, which obviously came from the public library.

The only other sound in the Hothouse was the babbling water. The caretaker watched them for a while, then retreated behind his bush. He had many subsequent opportunities to study the two absolutely silent gentlemen. Whichever of them arrived first would sit at one end of the bench. And when the other arrived, they would exchange a quick bow, always the same.

As soon as it was clear to Uncle that he wouldn't have to talk, his hostility gave way to a kind of unwilling respect. He had discovered that the library book was Spinoza, and that increased his esteem. He decided to bring a book himself to make an impression, and next day opened a bulky botanical work his family had given him. But the book was too heavy and cumbersome to hold in his lap and the print was much too small. Now and then the man beside Uncle, the intruder, would repeat in an undertone some phrase that appealed to him or disturbed him in his book, or he might say to himself that it was too hot or wonder why he couldn't ever have the bench to himself in peace... And on one occasion he said with contempt, "He knows nothing about flowers; he's just pretending."

This upset Uncle so badly that he threw caution to the winds, stood up and shouted, "You're the one who doesn't know a damn thing about flowers! You never even look at them! You should stay at home with your stupid books!"

"Astonishing," said his neighbour, removing his glasses. He studied Uncle with a certain interest. "If I understand correctly, you are also a man who values silence. My name is Josephson."

"Vesterberg," said Uncle crossly, retrieving his own book from the floor. He slammed it shut with a bang and sat down.

"And now," continued Josephson, "perhaps we can leave one another in peace. Or join one another in peace."

This was how their relationship began, grimly, and with few words.

It gradually emerged that Josephson lived in a noisy place called Peaceful Haven full of tiresome old gentlemen who wanted to talk. He mentioned this in passing and without comment. Uncle stopped bringing his botanical book with him. Now the tranquillity of the Hothouse was once again a place of meditation and peace, funnily enough an even greater peace than in the days when he'd had the bench to himself.

Then suddenly Josephson vanished; he didn't come to the Hothouse for a whole week. Uncle spoke to the caretaker, who knew nothing.

Maybe Josephson's ill, thought Uncle. I must find out.

The caretaker helped him find Peaceful Haven in the telephone catalogue. Telephoning was tiresome; Uncle kept being put through to the wrong department. In the end someone in the kitchen said Josephson was angry and didn't want to see anybody. She sounded very angry herself.

Peaceful Haven seemed quite dreadful to Uncle. He had never even imagined so much anxious old age gathered together in one place. At home, everyone else was much younger, so he was naturally an exception, almost unique, but here he felt himself absorbed into a compact anonymous mass. Suddenly he was no more than an insignificant part of the weary flotsam that life had washed ashore and forgotten. Someone showed him to Josephson's room, a very small room that seemed strangely empty. Josephson was lying in bed with the covers pulled up to his chin.

"Ah," said Josephson. "Vesterberg. I'm so grateful that you haven't brought flowers. In any case, I'm not ill, just bored stiff. Do sit down. Well, how's life with the lotus lover?"

"The caretaker sends his greetings," said Uncle, looking for somewhere to sit. Both chairs in the room were piled high with books.

"Just put them on the floor," said Josephson impatiently. "I'm tired of them. Nothing but words, all of them, words and words and words. They don't help. They're not enough." After a pause he continued, almost to himself. "Vesterberg, you let yourself be spoiled. And you don't understand what a great gift you've been given. Go on gazing at your blessed lotus blossoms; go on looking at them so long as there's time to look, and be grateful you've never felt any need to struggle towards an idea, I mean, search for something worth believing in and defending."

"I did once defend a meadow," Uncle began, but Josephson wasn't listening; he climbed out of bed and went to the bathroom.

My meadow, Uncle thought, the meadow I saved... But perhaps I shouldn't talk about that just now.

Josephson came back with two toothbrush glasses and a small bottle of cognac. He sat down on the edge of the bed and said, "Add water from the tap if you like. I prefer it neat."

"Are you coming back to the Hothouse?" said Uncle. "What excellent cognac!"

"This is the only brand worth drinking."

A bell rang in the corridor.

"Food," said Josephson with contempt. "What have you been up to?"

"Nothing much. But why are you tired of your books?"

"They break everything up. You know, Vesterberg, they drive me to despair by dividing things into tiny little trains of thought that lead nowhere. Nowhere for me, at any rate. They don't lead to what I need to know in order to understand. So I'm tired of them."

"Perhaps," said Uncle carefully. "Perhaps you should just let them be for a bit and try another way."

"What do you mean? What way?"

Uncle looked at Josephson and made a gesture which really could have meant anything at all, principally unavailing interest.

"In this place," said Josephson, "time is just something that passes; it is no longer alive. Any more than it is in those books. What I need is a clear picture and I haven't much time, a clear picture of what I've wanted and tried to do and what came of it all and what really matters. It's important. Searching out something that might have real meaning, some sort of answer. An ultimate, valid conclusion. Do you know what I mean?"

Uncle said, "Not really... But in the end does all that really matter? If all it does is upset you. And surely it's no more urgent now than it was before."

Josephson started to laugh. "Vesterberg," he said, "there's something very likeable about you. But you really are a great big donkey, aren't you?"

"Yes, of course," said Uncle. "But you will come back to the Hothouse, won't you?"

"Yes, yes. I'll come when I come. But for the moment I shan't say another word, not a single sensible word."

On his way home on the tram, Uncle did not think much about what had been said in this undoubtedly very meaningful if somewhat incomprehensible conversation. He thought only about Josephson himself and about his own meadow. Clearest was the image of the meadow, the meadow he had saved.

I must tell him about that meadow sometime, he thought.

* * *

The year before Uncle met Josephson, his relatives had hired a summer cottage on a skerry near the coast. Since the little island was covered with steep and difficult terrain, they worried about Uncle and spent a long time discussing whether it would be better to take him with them or leave him behind in the city. Uncle wasn't as deaf as he led them to believe and heard most of their discussions. In the end he laid out a game of patience as he sometimes did when faced with an important but difficult decision. If the patience came out it would mean stay, and if not it would mean go. It was a kind of patience that practically never came out.

The most characteristic feature of the island was a deep ravine cutting across it from west to east. The fisherman from whom they rented it had bridged the ravine with scrap wood so he wouldn't have to climb down to the meadow by the shore if he wanted to get from the dock to the cottage. The bridge was a ramshackle structure, but it did save a great deal of time.

The first time Uncle climbed the hill he suddenly stopped abruptly. The others thought he must be afraid of venturing out onto the bridge, but that wasn't it at all. He had caught sight of the meadow, which now in July was in full bloom, lightly and airily fluttering with the colours of all the different flowers that blossom in unison but last only a short time. He could see that no one had crossed the meadow; it was as untouched as on that first morning in paradise, and he thought it even more beautiful than the Hothouse. He decreed that no one should disturb the meadow. It was only to be seen.

Every day just before dawn Uncle slithered down the hillside to sit in a corner of his meadow. It was at its most beautiful at the moment when the sun rose above the horizon. Then, just for a short time, the colours would glow with an almost unearthly translucence. And the mild July winds would set the flower carpet billowing as if in a dance. What a sight! Uncle was not being unfaithful to the Hothouse; it was just that what is constantly changing is superior to what is static, and the meadow was full of life. Sometimes he felt the same dangerous desire he experienced in the Hothouse, as if his sense of wonder entitled him to walk right in and feel the meadow close around him, embrace it – but he held back.

Then one fine day the family decided to erect a tent sauna. Of course. Even the smallest cottage in Finland has its sauna. Now, a tent sauna must be set up on level ground, and the only level ground on the island was Uncle's meadow. Some difficult days followed, with strong words and long silences. But, as so often happens in families, a compromise was reached: the sauna would be built under the bridge, very discreetly and with the least possible disturbance to the meadow.

When they had erected their sauna under the bridge and gone away, Uncle came to have a look. It was a large square monstrosity with a metal chimney, a misshapen intrusion on the landscape. He went closer and opened the door flap. Inside it was dim, with broad wooden planks for benches, a stove filled with black stones, an iron kettle, a water bucket, and a storm lantern. A utilitarian, private place. Uncle sat down on the lowest bench. This caused the opening of the tent to frame his meadow so that suddenly it resembled a painting, very bright beyond the twilight in the tent. He almost felt he'd painted it himself.

No one was surprised when Uncle said he would like to sleep in the sauna. They fixed it up for him and carried down every imaginable thing he might want. He listened to them tramping across the bridge and it reminded him of the visitors to the Hothouse, the ones who climbed the spiral staircase only to tramp down again and go away.

It was nice living under the bridge, between its strong supporting pillars. The wood still smelt of tar and was full of old nails no one had taken the trouble to pull out. He hung his hat and stick on nails, also a hand towel and various other items – and remembered what it had been like sleeping in a tent when he was a child.

Then one night at the end of July the wind rose and high water swept through the ravine, flooding the meadow and gradually invading Uncle's tent sauna. He woke up to find himself on a wet mattress, not quite sure where he was. The tent fluttered and slapped and it was too hot, as hot and damp as the Hothouse – a storm over the lily pond... A mass of odd objects were floating about on the water. Uncle pushed them aside and waded out into the wet night, fascinated.

Outside it was lighter; he could make out the glass cupola above the long dark swells rolling through the ravine. The cupola was much higher than usual, in fact it never stopped, and the spiral staircase had vanished. Uncle unhooked his stick from its nail and stood still, listening to the wind. The meadow billowed anxiously to and fro around him as he stumbled on. Yes, now at last he could embrace the meadow, walk straight into the lotus pond, feel soft elastic soil under his bare feet and the gentle touch of waterlilies – and he could understand the hitherto unimaginable battle of innocent flowers against an aggressive sea... No visitors today, not a single one, he was alone, free to possess what he loved, calm and untroubled.

Gradually he made his way up to the cottage and fell asleep. So he didn't see the tent sauna carried off at dawn, flapping away like a ragged bat. He didn't see the bridge's strong legs give way and bulge and break, the splintered wood tossed high in the air and swept aside by the angry sea.

By the time the last fragments of the bridge had gone, the ravine was a torrent of raging water.

A bit of the bridge caught fast in a crevice on the far side of the island and was chopped up for firewood. The rest, swept out to sea, eventually washed up as flotsam on other shores, where it was found and used for a shed or a dock; it would all be made useful one way or another.

The family built a new bridge across the ravine, in Uncle's opinion an eyesore. It wasn't a proper bridge but looked more like a level crossing on a railway, a sort of varnished wooden platform that had nothing to do with him or the meadow. The old bridge had been weathered by sun and salt water and had taken on the colours of the hillside; it had blended with the land and become a natural part of the structure of the island. But Uncle said nothing, because they were all so proud of the mess they had made.

The meadow did not recover from the night of the great storm but he knew that next July it would be just as beautiful as before. And they'd done battle against the sea, he and the meadow together.

One day Uncle noticed their firewood was grey and full of nails, lumber from the old bridge. He chose some suitable pieces and found the tools he needed. Slowly, with the great care, he began making a tiny copy of the old bridge that looked just like the original.

* * *

When Uncle visited the Hothouse after his visit to Peaceful Haven, Josephson was back on his old perch.

He put down his book and said, "Well, Vesterberg, you old hedonist, good to see you. As you see I'm still search-ing for some sort of logic that makes sense. But these writers are no smarter than they ever were."

He made room on the bench and went on reading. Uncle sat down on his own side, the left; it was nice to have Josephson back. Uncle thought about telling him about the meadow and the storm, but the time still didn't seem right. So he just sat gazing at the beautiful lily pond, which suddenly seemed altered. He closed his eyes and tried to see farther, deeper, and was embraced once again by the dark resistance of the water and the softly billowing meadow.

They continued coming to the Hothouse, though not so often as before. The caretaker who used to sit behind the bush with his crochet work had retired. The new one, who did not know them, preferred a table inside the main entrance and would slowly walk round the lily pond from time to time, round and round, his hands behind his back. He would pass right in front of their bench with no sign of respect or recognition.

Josephson seemed perfectly happy to be left in silence, occasionally exchanging the odd word, stretching his legs, underlining a sentence in his book. Every time Uncle let the silence stretch out, he grew more uneasy and annoyed. He had begun to bring the model bridge with him every day but it became harder and harder to show it and tell the story of the night of the storm; he simply couldn't do it. The night when he embraced the meadow was slipping away from him, and Josephson was no help at all.

Then one day as they were sitting in the Hothouse as usual, a furious thunderstorm blew in over the city. Day turned to twilight, rain pelted the glass cupola, and in the thunder and lightning Josephson, his book held close under his nose, could hardly see to read. A heavy squall threw open the Hothouse doors; there was a crash of glass and the storm burst in, making waves in the lily pond – tiny waves, but waves nonetheless. Uncle stood up, walked forward and waded straight into the pool, shoving aside leaves and lilies regardless, then turned and called out, "Josephson! Do you see what I'm doing?"

"Good," said Josephson, putting down his book. "Keep at it. Very stimulating."

Later they sat together till closing time. The storm had gradually subsided and the caretaker calmed down. Uncle talked about the meadow and talked very well. Josephson was a better listener than he could have expected. Uncle showed him the little bridge. He looked at Uncle and said, "Yes, yes, I understand. The essence of the meadow. See, admire, experience, all that. And the bridge – what's the point of a bridge that doesn't lead anywhere?"

"It doesn't mean anything," said Uncle angrily. "A bridge is a bridge is a bridge, just a bridge. Here you are again trying to find meaning in something that's just obvious. Where it goes and where it comes from doesn't matter. You just go over it, and that's all there is to it!"

The caretaker came over and suggested that Uncle go home before he caught cold.

"We're having a conversation," said Uncle. "Josephson, have you reached any conclusion? Have you found anything important in those books?"

"This and that," said Josephson, smiling. "It takes time, but I always knew it would. It looks as if neither of us will ever convince the other. But do we need to?"

"No," said Uncle. "The other person only needs to listen and understand."

"I can accept that," said Josephson. "I liked that part about the meadow."

Uncle said, "Yes, I do think I told it rather well."

They stood up together and went out through the Hothouse's storm-shattered doors, and after a friendly word separated and each made his own way home.

Correspondence

Dear Jansson san

I'm a girl from Japan.
I'm thirteen years old and two months.
On the eighth of January I'll be fourteen.
I have a mother and two little sisters.
I've read everything you've written.
When I've read something I read it one more time.
Then I think about snow and how to be alone.
Tokyo's a very big city.
I'm learning English and studying very seriously.
I love you.
I dream one day I'll be as old as you and as clever as
    you.
I have many dreams.
There's a Japanese kind of poem called haiku.
I'm sending you a haiku in Japanese
It's about cherry flowers.
Do you live in a big forest?

Forgive me for writing to you.
I wish you good health and a long life.
Tamiko Atsumi

Dear Jansson san

My new birthday today is very important.
Your present is very important to me.
Everyone admires your present and the picture of the
    little island where you live.
It's hanging above my bed.
How many lonely islands are there in Finland?
Can anyone live there who wants to?
I want to live on an island.
I love lonely islands and I love flowers and snow.
But I can't write how they are.
I'm studying very seriously.
I read your books in English.
Your books aren't the same in Japanese.
Why are they different?
I think you are happy.
Look after your health very carefully.

I wish you a long life.
Tamiko Atsumi

Dear Jansson san

It's been a long time, for five months and nine days you
    haven't written to me.
Did you get my letters?
Did you get the presents?
I long for you.
You must understand that I'm studying very seriously.
Now I'll tell you about my dream.
My dream is to travel to other countries and learn their
    languages and learn to understand.
I want to be able to talk with you.
I want you to talk with me.
You must tell me how you describe things without
    seeing other houses and with no one getting in the way.
I want to know how to write about snow.
I want to sit at your feet and learn.
I'm collecting money so I can travel.
Now I'm sending you a new haiku.
It's about a very old woman who sees blue mountains far
    away.
When she was young she didn't see them.
Now she can't reach them.
That's a beautiful haiku.

I beg you please be careful.
Tamiko

Dear Jansson san

You were going to go on a great long journey, now
    you've been travelling more than six months.
I think you've come back again.
Where did you go, my Jansson san, and what did you
    learn on your journey?
Perhaps you took with you a kimono.
In autumn colours and autumn is the time to travel.
But you've said so often that time is short.
My time grows long when I think of you.
I want to become old like you and have only big
    clever thoughts.
I keep your letters in a very beautiful box in a
    secret place.
I read them again at sundown.

Tamiko

Dear Jansson san

Once you wrote to me when it was summer in Finland
    and you were living on the lonely island.
You've told me that post hardly ever comes to your
    island.
Then do you get many letters from me at once?
You say it feels nice when the ships go by and
    don't stop.

But now it's winter in Finland.
You've written a book about winter, you've
    described my dream.
I'll write a story to help everyone understand and
    recognise their own dream.
How old must you be to write a story?
But I can't write my story without you.
Every day is a day of waiting.
You've said you're so tired.
You work and there are too many people.
But I want to be the one who comforts you and
    protects your solitude.
This is a sad haiku about someone who waited too
    long for the one they loved.
You see how it went!
But it's not so good in translation.
Has my English got any better?

Always
Tamiko

Much loved Jansson san, thank you!

Yes, that's how it is, you don't have to be a certain age,
you just begin writing a story because you have
to, about what you know or also about what you long
for, about your dream, the unknown. O much loved
Jansson san. One mustn't worry about others and
what they think and understand, because while you're

telling a story you're only concerned with the story and yourself. Then you really are on your own. At this moment I know all about what it's like to love someone far away and I will hurry to write about it before she comes nearer. I send you a haiku again, it's about a little stream which becomes happy in spring so everyone listens and feels delight. I can't translate it.

Listen to me Jansson san and write to say when I can come. I've collected money and I think I'll get a travel scholarship. What month would be best and most beautiful for our meeting?

Tamiko

Dear Jansson san

Thank you for your very wise letter.
I understand the forest's big in Finland and the sea
    too but your house is very small.
It's a beautiful thought, to meet a writer only in
    her books.
I'm learning all the time.

I wish you good health and a long life.
Your Tamiko Atsumi

My Jansson san

It's been snowing all day.
I'm learning to write about snow.
Today my mother died.
When you're the eldest in your family in Japan, you
    can't leave home and don't want to.
I hope you understand me.
I thank you.
The poem is by Lang Shih Yiian, who was once a
    great poet in China.
It has been translated into your language by Hwang
    Tsu-Yii and Alf Henrikson.
"Wild geese scream shrilly on muffled winds.
The morning snow is heavy, weather cloudy and cold.
Poor, I can give you nothing in parting
but the blue mountains and they'll always be with you."

Tamiko

Tove Jansson | fair play

A book about love – tender, eccentric and fiercely independent. It feels a privilege to read it.' *Esther Freud*

....

So what can happen when Tove Jansson turns her attention to her own favourite subjects, love and work, in this novel about two women, lifelong partners and friends? Expect something philosophically calm – and discreetly radical. Its publication is cause for huge celebration. (From Ali Smith's introduction to *Fair Play*).

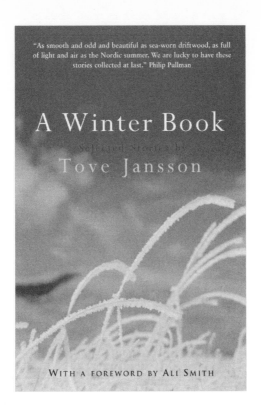

"As smooth and odd and beautiful as sea-worn driftwood, as full of light and air as the Nordic summer. We are lucky to have these stories collected at last." Philip Pullman

A Winter Book

Selected Stories by

Tove Jansson

WITH A FOREWORD BY ALI SMITH

Written with such a lightness of touch that it seems miraculous, these stories are a further revelation of Tove Jansson's heart warming genius. *Ali Smith*

··

A *Winter Book* collection of some of Tove Jansson's best loved and most famous stories. Drawn from youth and older age, and spanning most of the twentieth century, this newly translated selection provides a thrilling showcase of the great Finnish writer's prose, scattered with insights and home truths. It has been selected and is introduced by Ali Smith.

Tove Jansson was a genius. This is a marvellous, beautiful, wise novel, which is also very funny. *Philip Pullman*

···

An elderly artist and her six-year-old granddaughter while away a summer together on a tiny island in the gulf of Finland. Gradually, the two learn to adjust to each other's fears, whim and yearnings for independence, and a fierce yet understated love emerges – one that encompasses not only the summer inhabitants but the island itself, with its mossy rocks, windswept firs and unpredictable seas. Full of brusque humour and wisdom, *The Summer Book* is a profoundly life-affirming story.